Too Young

"I love you, Craddoc," I said, my voice sounding like a recording in my ears.

He gathered me close, and as we sat staring at the feathery outlines of the cedar trees, his words came dreamily into the night. "It seems like I've waited forever. I knew you were too young at fifteen. I thought maybe sixteen. Then my mother said you were a young sixteen."

"You talked this over with your mother?"

"No, she just happened to say that you were a smart, but a young, sixteen."

That didn't make me feel too great.

His arms tightened around me. "Anyway, I thought, When she's seventeen. That will be OK. That will be the time. What do you think?"

I wasn't about to admit I was a young seventeen. I mumbled that I didn't know.

His body sagged. "Don't you want me?"

"Any girl would want you, Craddoc." I reached up and stroked his face, trying to erase the hurt reflected in his voice.

Seventeen &
In-Between

Barthe DeClements

SCHOLASTIC INC.
New York Toronto London Auckland Sydney

0-590-33559-6

Copyright © 1984 by Barthe DeClements and Christopher Greimes. All rights reserved. Published by Scholastic Inc., 730 Broadway, New York, NY 10003, by arrangement with Viking Penguin, Inc.

12 11 10 9 8 7 6 5 4 3 2 1   10   5 6 7 8 9/8 0/9

Printed in the U.S.A.   01

I would like to thank my son, Christopher Greimes, for writing the letters from Jack in this book, and for collaborating with me on the scenes involving Jack's Christmas visit, New Year's Eve, and Elsie's visit to Kalaloch.

I give special thanks to my daughter, Nicole Southard, for her critique of the manuscript in progress.

Seventeen &
In-Between

CONTENTS

1. Double F

Explaining computers to Jenny was about as easy as explaining fractions to her when we were in the fifth grade. I think the wheels of her brain lock at the sound of numbers. I tried again. "Robyn's Atari and the practice computers in the math room don't need passwords. But the computer in the attendance office and the ones in the counselors' offices are hooked up to the main computer in Olson's office, where all the data is stored. So these computers need passwords. Got it?"

"Got it," she said.

I waited until I had driven through mass traffic at the 44th Street light in Lynnwood before I went on. "So all Rick Evers has to do is learn the passwords to get into the student records stored in the main computer."

"And that's easy?"

I turned off 44th and went down the street to my house. "It isn't easy, because the passwords never show on the monitors, but both he and Darrel were standing behind the senior counselor watching her fingers while she worked her keyboard."

"Darrel's such a fat pig," Jenny said.

"Fat pig" sent an old stripe of pain into my stomach. Jenny and I are longtime friends, and I guess she picked that up. I felt her glance at me quickly.

"It seems ages since you were fat. You're so thin now. You were never a jerk like Darrel, though."

"No?" I pulled up in front of my house. "I only stole all the kids' lunch money to stuff candy in my face."

"Well . . . with good reason."

My dog, Honey Bear, met me at the car door and followed us up the front steps.

"I wonder what Jack's doing now," I said, reaching down to pet Honey Bear. "I've been thinking about him all day long."

"He shouldn't have dropped out of school," Jenny said.

"I don't know about that. He told me once that school never did anything for him, and he was probably right."

My sister, Robyn, was sitting at the table reading the mail when we got into the kitchen. I took a Diet Dr Pepper out of the refrigerator for me and a Coke for Jenny. We sat down with Robyn and asked her how it was going.

"OK. I got an invitation to a party Friday night." Robyn pushed two envelopes toward me from the pile in front of her. "You got letters from Jack and Craddoc."

"A letter from Jack? Aw right!" I ripped open the envelope, and Jenny and Robyn crowded in close to read along with me.

Hello Elsie,

Sorry I took so long to write you after I left. I wanted to get myself set up with a job before I wrote anybody at home. When I left, things were a little tense. Mom wanted me to go back to school, and Dad wanted me to go to school or get a job. My brother Kevin told me I could stay with him and Lisa in Clearwater for a while. (I just had to get out of that house.)

Anyway, I got a job, a good job! I'm packing shakes in the mill Kevin works in. What are shakes? Shakes are made out of cedar and used for roofing. Diane's got them on her roof. I get paid 22¢ a bundle. Yesterday I packed 203 and made $44.66. That's more than I ever thought I would make on my first job. I tried to get a job splitting cedar blocks in the woods with this guy named Grover who lives next door to Kevin. He turned me down because he doesn't think I can handle it. It pisses me off because I know I could do it if he'd just let me try.

Well, I'd better go to bed now. We have to be at work by 7:00, which means we have to get up before 6:00. A little bit

*hard to get used to but I'm doing it.
Write back soon.*

Take care,
Jack

*P.S. I met this really interesting guy,
named Steve Four-Suns. He's the Shaman of the Indians around here. I guess
the Shaman of the tribe is like the
medicine man. He doesn't look like any
medicine man I've ever seen but he sure
has real nice vibes. I told him I might be
forced into going back to school if I
couldn't get a job. He told me this: If a
person doesn't make his own decisions,
his decisions will be made for him. He
said the trick is to become cause instead
of effect. Kind of interesting, huh?*

"Forty-four times five is two hundred and
twenty. That, times four and a half," Robyn
figured, "is almost a thousand a month.
Maybe you'd better turn Craddoc in for Jack,
Elsie."

"Nooo, Jack's just a friend."

"You went out with him when you were a
freshman, didn't you?" Robyn asked Jenny.

"Off and on. Before I met Einer. But Jack
probably just hung around me to be near
Elsie."

"Where's Clearwater?" I wondered.

"Over near Forks, I think." Robyn got up.
"I'll get the map out of your glove compart-
ment."

We all pored over the Washington State

map when Robyn brought it back. Clearwater was on the other side of the Olympic Mountains, south of Forks.

Robyn traced the red highway line from Lynnwood to Aberdeen and then up near Clearwater. "Must be about three or four hours from here. Whoa, it's near the Rain Forest and the Hoh River. That's where Cecile's brother goes to pick mushrooms. His mother heard him and his friends talking about making the trip once, and she told him to bring some of the mushrooms home and she'd cook them with steaks."

I took a good look at Robyn while she giggled, her dark eyes shining in her pixie face. She was growing up, no doubt.

Then she got serious. "Hey, I wanted to ask you something. The party Friday night is in Nicole's basement and her dad's probably going to play poker that night."

"And leave all you JH's alone?" Jenny said.

"Their rec room's totaled anyway," Robyn said. "But what I want to know. . . . You two get around, sooo. . . . Well, this time some guys I know might be there and how about how I should act?"

Jenny and I thought that one over.

"Come on, Elsie," Robyn said.

"OK." I paced it out carefully. "If someone spikes the punch, don't get too drunk, don't leave with strange guys, and don't ride in a car with a drunk driver."

"That's all?" Robyn asked.

Jenny nodded. "That's about it."

"But that's what I was wondering about . . . what if a boy . . . uh . . . wants to fool around or something?"

"You're on your own there," I told her. "Only, like Jack said, if you don't make your own decision, someone else will make it for you."

"And the boys will be delighted to," Jenny added.

"Well, what do you and Craddoc do?" Robyn persisted. "Have you done everything?"

"You're only thirteen, Robyn. And this is just a party."

"I know that, but have you?"

"No," I said.

"Why not? You've been going with him for almost three years, ever since you were fourteen."

"I don't know." I shrugged. "Craddoc hasn't made a big issue out of it, I guess."

Robyn narrowed her eyes. "I thought you said you made your own decisions."

Jenny stood up, laughing. "I gotta go home and get dinner. See ya later."

After Jenny left I reminded Robyn it was her turn to make dinner at our house and I headed for my bedroom.

"Aren't you going to read Craddoc's letter?" she called after me.

"Oh, yes." I came back into the kitchen to get it. I loved Craddoc but I knew his letter would be a play-by-play account of his last football game.

It was. He also said he'd be home for Thanksgiving.

When I got into bed that night, I lay there wondering if I should invite Craddoc to my house for Thanksgiving dinner this year. I'd never cooked a turkey. I could make pies. Probably not as good as his mother, though. Robyn would help. I wondered if my mother would.

And what was I going to do about Rick Evers? Just say nothing even if he changed his grade on the computer? And what if he and Darrel changed other kids' grades?

Jack and I have a kind of telepathic bond and I missed talking to him. I got out of bed to do the next best thing, talk to him on paper.

Dear Jack,

I've been trying to go to sleep for an hour but all I've managed to do is wind up my top sheet. I just sat up in bed, trying to straighten it out, when I decided to bag bed, get some hot milk, and write to you.

I was going to start my letter out saying it was a big surprise to hear from you. I don't think it was. Well, maybe getting the letter was a surprise, but you'd been flitting in and out of my mind all afternoon.

The reason I can't sleep is because I'm shook up over what happened at school today. You remember that second period I'm assistant to Olson, who's the VP in charge of the school's computer system? Well, Olson has Mrs. Tabbs putting all the information from the students' permanent records onto the computer and he's going to do away with paper files. He thinks storing everything in the computer is a great idea. Efficient and all that.

And you remember Rick Evers, Fircrest's football hero since Craddoc graduated? He stopped me in the hall today and said he'd heard I was a computer genius. I mumbled something about liking math but if there was a computer genius in the school it was Darrel Norrison, not me. Rick gives me his big jock smile and says I work on the main computer, don't I? And he wonders if I'll do him a little favor. He asks me if I know that the athletic code says a student can't flunk two classes one quarter and play in games the next quarter.

I forgot about his macho pride and said, "You flunked two classes? How did you manage that?"

His jaw got all red but he tried to carry on like flunking two classes was no big deal. Anyway, he wanted me to change one of his flunks to a withdrawal so he could win the WESCO championship for Fircrest. When I told him no way, he leans on me a bit and says since I was Craddoc's girl and he was Craddoc's old teammate he thought I'd want to help him out and it wasn't like asking for a grade or a credit. He was going to drop the class, so it wouldn't make any difference if I changed his F to a W on the computer. If I'd just do that little thing, when the coach asked for a printout of the team's grades, Rick'd still be eligible to play. Right?

Wrong!

I was late to second period. Olson didn't notice because he was hopping around the computer room while the printer cranked out a schedule for a new kid. "Isn't this beautiful, Elsie? Think of the time it saves. The counselors just type in one schedule, push the print button on one of their computers, and the printer in here prints out a copy for the student. As soon as Mrs. Tabbs finishes the last file drawer of permanent records, we'll have the janitor wheel away the old metal file cabinets, and no more paper trail. Isn't that beautiful, Elsie?"

Sure.

While he was still glowing over the marvels of high tech, I took the new kid's schedule down to the counselors' area. Guess who was standing behind the senior counselor while she recorded a drop on her machine? Rick Evers and Darrel Norrison. Rick is fast! He was looking sooo innocent as he thanked her for her help. "Oh, while we're here," he said, "Darrel wants to know how many absences he has in calculus, if it isn't too much bother to turn on your computer again."

Darrel and Rick concentrated on the keyboard as the counselor pecked in the password to get back into the student menu. I put the schedule on her desk and got out of there.

Jack, I know Darrel will get the passwords and Rick will flatter him into figuring out some way to get at the main computer. What's keeping me from sleeping is, what do I do? I remember you didn't even nark on me in the fifth grade when I hit you in the mouth with a baseball bat. But I didn't know you were so close behind me when I swung the bat. And Rick knows what he's doing.

Awk! Now I've drunk so much hot milk I won't be able to sleep because I'll have to go to the bathroom all night.

What do you think I should do about Rick? Does your Shaman have any wise words? Jenny and I have already used his last wise words on Robyn, telling her she'd better make her mind up about what she wants to do about boys and sex or the boys will be happy to make the decision for her.

I really miss having you around to talk to. I guess you can see that by the length of this letter, huh?

'Night now,
Elsie

2. Stinking Animal

I saw Rick Evers in the school cafeteria when Jenny and I were having lunch the next day. I was at the relish table slopping tartar sauce on my fish sandwich when he and a friend came up. They didn't notice me because their attention was on a redheaded girl emptying her tray into one of the garbage cans. I couldn't hear what Rick's friend said about her, but Rick replied, "She's just a stinking animal. She'll sleep with anybody."

When I sat back down next to Jenny, I pointed out the redhead leaving the cafeteria.

"That's Tessie Jones," Jenny said. "Why?"

I concentrated on licking the sauce oozing from the sides of my bun. I didn't really want to repeat what Rick Evers had said about Tessie. The years people had hated me still hurt so bad I cringed when I felt it happening to someone else.

Jenny watched the girl push the bar across an exit door and disappear into the commons hall.

"She's sort of cute," I said.

"She'd look a lot cuter if she'd wash her hair," Jenny said, and went back to eating her cherry crisp.

As we left the cafeteria Jenny asked if I wanted to go to the Alderwood Mall after school to do some Christmas shopping before the crowds started.

"Maybe Friday," I said. "I've got too much math analysis to do tonight."

"I don't see how you stand that stuff."

"Actually, I find it pretty interesting," I told her.

Mother came home for dinner, which was unusual. She even made it, which was more unusual. She was in such a good mood Robyn and I locked questioning glances while Mother put a big platter of spaghetti in front of us. "New boyfriend?" Robyn mouthed silently to me.

While Mother was smoking a cigarette at the end of the meal, I brought up my idea of having Craddoc over to our house for Thanksgiving dinner.

"Great!" Robyn said. "And I'll invite Joe."

"Who's Joe?" Mother and I said together.

"Oh . . . just a friend," Robyn weaseled.

"Uh . . . I might invite a friend, too," Mother said.

Robyn passed me a smug look. "The best part of having Thanksgiving here is we get out of hauling Grandma to a restaurant." She got up to start clearing the dishes away.

Mother tapped her cigarette on the ash-tray. "We'll have to invite her, too."

Robyn stopped, an empty cup hanging in her hand. "What? Why? She's spoiled every holiday with her whining as long as I can remember. Why does she have to spoil this one?"

Mother shrugged. "We're the only family she has here."

"Tell her to visit Uncle Harold in California this year. Let her drag down their fun for a change. She thinks Uncle Harold is so perfect, anyway."

"I might do that," Mother considered.

Robyn put the cup and silverware on the counter and sat back down at the table. "Listen, Elsie, let's have a big spread. Turkey, dressing, mashed potatoes, mince pies — the whole works."

"I don't know how to make mince pies, only pumpkin pies," I said.

"I'll make the mince pies," Mother offered.

"And I'll make the mashed potatoes and candied sweet potatoes," Robyn planned. "Have you asked Craddoc yet?"

"No," I said. "I thought I'd write and invite him."

"Do it now. Do it now!" Robyn jumped up. "I'll do the dishes and you go to your room and write him and tell him to call you as soon as he gets your letter so we'll have time to get everything together. Thanksgiving's only a little over a week away, you know."

While I was walking toward my bedroom,

I heard Mother tell Robyn, "You could candy the sweet potatoes Saturday and freeze them, so there'd be less to do Thanksgiving morning. And I could make the dressing ahead, too, and freeze it."

In the middle of my letter to Craddoc, I stopped and gazed at the rain dribbling down the outside of the dark windowpane. I wished I lived in a place where it snowed all winter instead of raining most of the time. Just the same, this would be a happy Thanksgiving. We were such a little family, holidays never seemed like much. Mother had never made them much, either. Not like Craddoc's mom did.

On the ride to school next morning, I told Jenny I'd take her shopping Friday afternoon.

Friday started out to be a prime day. I'd bought a new navy-blue turtleneck and was wearing it with my jeans. Before second period I stopped in the girls' lavatory, and on my way out I caught reflections of myself in the wide mirror. The sweater seemed to make my eyes look bluer. There was only one thing about navy wool. I turned around to be sure no long curly blond hairs were sticking to the back of it.

Tessie Jones was in the john, too. She was plastering another coat of lipstick on her mouth. Jenny was right. She *could* wash her hair. Her whole self, for that matter.

Mr. Olson and the janitor were talking in

the computer room when I got there. The janitor was holding a black box. I asked Mr. Olson what the box was after the janitor left.

"That's an electric eye. We place it around the school, nights and weekends, for surveillance. If the beam's broken, 'Burglary in progress at Fircrest High' repeats in the police cars."

I was thinking fast and trying to act casual at the same time. "Maybe you should put it outside the computer room this weekend."

"Why's that?" He gave me a sharp look.

"Well . . . uh . . . the quarter grades are out."

"Do you know anybody who would break in here to try to change their grades without knowing the passwords?" Friendly Mr. Olson had turned into a vice principal and I started to sweat.

I was the only student allowed to have the passwords into the computer and word processing. Actually, I knew the password for the student records, too, because I had overheard Mrs. Tabbs teaching the counselors, but I didn't think Mr. Olson knew that. I waved my hands around helplessly. "I don't know . . . I just thought. . . ."

Luckily for me, about this time Mrs. Tabbs came into the room to say there was a parent waiting to see Mr. Olson in his office. I felt miserable the rest of the day and didn't lighten up until I unloaded the scene on Jenny while we were riding to Alderwood Mall.

"I don't think Rick would actually break

into the school," Jenny told me. "He has too much at stake. This is his senior year and the colleges will be scouting him."

"That's true," I said. It was true. Probably he and Darrel would only try to slip into one of the counselors' offices when they were at a meeting. And that would be hard because kids and secretaries were going in and out of that area all the time.

I parked my car in front of Nordstroms'. As we piled out, Jenny sighed. "You're so lucky. I wish I had a little MG."

"What was lucky about baby-sitting Jeanne and Dad's kid ten hours a day for two solid summers while everyone else was down at the beach?"

"Ya. Hmmm." Jenny pushed Nordstroms' glass door open. "Seems like your mom would have given you a better price."

"She charged me what she could get on a turn-in for her new car. She said she thought I'd want it on a 'businesslike basis.'"

We wandered over to the accessories counter and Jenny wrapped a red silk scarf around her neck. I tilted my head to pick up the effect. "That looks good with your brown eyes and brown hair."

Jenny examined the price tag. "Twenty-five dollars!" She dropped the scarf back on the counter.

We moved over to purses.

A gray leather shoulder bag was hanging from a stand on the counter. I took it down. It was buttery soft, part smooth leather and part suede. "This would look great on my mother."

"I bet it's fifty dollars," Jenny said.

I opened the clasp and took out the tag. "You're right, fifty dollars." I was reluctant to give up the purse, though, and stood there stroking its sides.

"Have you got fifty dollars?" Jenny said finally.

"Yes, but. I've got to get Robyn a present and Craddoc and Grandma and. . . ." I placed the purse back on its hanger.

We rode the escalator up to the third-floor gift shop and browsed around until Jenny found a bud vase she thought would be perfect for her mother's roses. When we were on the way back down the stairs, my mind clamped on the gray purse. I'd have to babysit most every weekend till Christmas to cover my other presents, but it was worth it. Jenny stood around with a disapproving look on her face while I bought the purse and had it gift-wrapped.

"Gawd, you're extravagant," she said as we scurried out to my car in the rain.

"I know, but I hardly ever find anything I'm sure she will like."

"She's always been such a bitch to you, I don't know how you can even spend five dollars on her."

I unlocked the car doors and dropped my package behind the seat. "She's not so bad anymore."

"Only because she knows you'll take off and

live with your dad if she pulls any of the crap she used to pull."

We didn't say much on the ride to Jenny's house. I was thinking about my mother and I guess she was, too.

"It's funny," Jenny said after I pulled up to her parking strip. "You're driving the car your mom wouldn't let you ride in when you were in the fifth grade." She gathered up her books and her mother's Christmas present, yanked the hood of her jacket up to protect her hair from the rain, said thank you, see ya, and dashed for her doorway.

I eased the MG out into the road slowly. Jenny was so raspy lately and I didn't know why. She was right about my mother, though. My mother had liked me, I think, when I was little, before Robyn was born. I was a miniature replica of my mother then, plump and blond. I remember her holding my hand in front of the bathroom mirror as we admired ourselves in the twin dresses she had made us. Then, sometime after Robyn, my dad began to spend his evenings with other ladies. A scene from that time is filed in my brain.

I remember that dinnertime had come and gone. Still, Mother rocked Robyn, tears streaming down her face. I stood on my tiptoes and bent over the baby, trying to reach up to brush the tears away. Mother elbowed me crossly and told me to go find something to do.

"I'm hungry," I whined.

"Go get some cookies out of the cookie jar, then."

The cookie jar became my friend, my comforter. And after Dad and Mother divorced, I ballooned as Mother shrank. At first, maybe I reminded her of what had been and she didn't want me around. Later, as she became slim and svelte and I grew grosser and grosser, I think she was ashamed of me and found ways to keep me away from her, like having a sports car that only took two, Robyn and her. I was old enough to stay home by myself.

I was the target of her frustrations until I was fifteen. That was after the diets had finally worked and I had Jenny and Jack for friends and Craddoc for love. Even though the damage no longer showed on the outside, the years with Mother had set my head up to expect rejection. My endless suspicions depressed Craddoc, and to keep him, I worked on my head until I could stand up to my mother. When I threatened to move in with my dad, she gave me a stinging slap, for which she apologized later. The apology — a first — didn't melt an inch of the ice that had replaced my fear of her.

But it *was* funny, I thought as I turned down my street, that the car I was driving was the same one I never got to ride in when I was in grade school. It was funny, too, that Mother acted so nice lately. And Jenny so raspy.

3. The Pill

When I arrived home, Robyn was in the bathroom curling her eyelashes and swearing.

"Robyn!" I said.

She eyed me through the curler. "I haven't got long, curly lashes like you have, Elsie, so back off."

"Robyn!"

"Well" — she turned to the mirror — "I pinched my skin, and now my eyelid will be all red and puffy for the party."

I piled my books, package, and purse on the toilet seat. "Here, let me see."

She opened the curler and leaned toward me.

"There's only a small red spot. Put some cold water on it and it will disappear."

She looked at me as if I were nuts. "Cold water! If I do that, my lashes will go all straight again."

"Put a little ice on it, then." I gathered up my stuff. "When's dinner?"

"Oh, you make it, Elsie. Please. Then I'll

make it two days in a row. I still have to do my hair, and Cecile's coming at eight."

"It's only six o'clock."

"I know, but you do it, OK?"

"OK," I said. "This Joe going to be there?"

Her cheeks flushed. "Yes."

I stood looking at her. "Hmmm."

She put the curler down and reached for a new tube of brown mascara. "Mom called and said she's showing some people an apartment complex and she might not be home to take us to the party, so will you drive us? Cecile's mom is picking us up."

"There isn't room for both you and Cecile in my car."

"I know, but we can stuff in and it's only a little way to Nicole's house."

I thought that one over. I didn't want to get a ticket and raise my insurance, but this party was obviously a big deal to Robyn. "Have you got gas money?"

"It's only a little way, Elsie."

"Have you got gas money?"

"I'll get it."

At eight-forty-five, after Robyn had changed her whole outfit because Cecile was wearing jeans, the two were finally ready. They bounced out to the car looking like TV models for Levi's, Robyn with her brown eyes and shining cap of blond hair and Cecile with her almond eyes and curly red hair, which always reminded me of Jack's.

Turning the ignition key, I warned them,

"Now sit still so you don't knock the gear-shift."

"You sound like Cecile's mother," Robyn said. "She's always ragging about something."

"Really," Cecile agreed.

"Remember when we were going to TP Gerald's house?" Robyn said, squirming under Cecile's weight. "And your mother caught us going out the door with the toilet paper and we explained that it was for Gerald's house and she wanted to know why they couldn't afford their own toilet paper?"

"And remember" — Cecile laughed, bouncing on Robyn — "when we heard one of the guys call you a fox and she thought that meant you were in heat all the time? She wasn't going to let us be friends anymore until I explained to her that foxes weren't the same as minxes."

Robyn giggled. "Your mom's always playing the wrong game upstairs."

"Really," Cecile said.

They piled out of the car at Nicole's house and fluffed their hair and licked their lips. Cecile handed me two dollars for gas before they went giggling and shoving each other up Nicole's steps. I felt graspy taking money for such a short ride, but with my splurge on the gray purse I couldn't be giving anything away.

I waited around the house all evening for Craddoc to phone. He didn't. Jeanne, Dad's wife, was the only one who did. She wanted me to baby-sit Saturday night. I said sure.

Craddoc called Saturday morning. When Robyn hollered, *"Phone!"* I'd barely gotten out of the shower. She was padding around the house in her pajamas, looking kind of pale after her big night. She and Mother were eating breakfast in the kitchen, I guess, but that didn't stop her from going through the living room several times while I was talking to Craddoc.

Craddoc was a perfect ass about the Thanksgiving dinner.

"But why can't we eat here for once?" I asked him. "We've been at your house for the last two years."

He went on about his mother's plans and about his being an only child. I felt like saying he was acting like one, too, but that was one of the times Robyn was moseying past, so I tried logic.

"Why don't you tell your mother that we'll have Christmas dinner at your house and Thanksgiving dinner here this year, OK?" I kept my voice sugary-sweet.

"Elsie." Craddoc wasn't even trying to hide his impatience. "Holiday dinners are a big thing in my family. They've never been, in yours."

"And why can't this year be a first for us?" I snapped. "I'd like to have pretty dishes on our dining-room table, for a change."

"Come on, Elsie, it's too late now. Thanksgiving's only four days away and my mom's probably been baking for a week."

I mumbled a four-letter word into the phone, knowing it was no use trying to buck Craddoc.

"What?" Craddoc said.

"Nothing," I told him.

"I kicked the extra point in the game yesterday. So we won."

"Good for you."

"You don't sound as if you think it was good."

"I'm sure it was," I told him. "We better hang up. You've probably used up all your quarters now."

"Just about," he agreed. "Hey, I love you."

"Me, too," I said and hung up the phone.

When I came into the kitchen, Robyn was fiddling with the remains of the Eggo waffle on her plate. "You couldn't talk him into it, huh?"

I got myself some grape juice out of the refrigerator and sat down with her and Mother. "No. Sometimes I think being an only child gave Craddoc a bigger problem than I had."

Mother looked up quickly. "What problem have you had?"

You, I almost said, but didn't. I shrugged instead and drank my grape juice.

"So much for freezing sweet potatoes today," Robyn said, picking up her plate. "We might as well have them for dinner. It's back to a restaurant with Grandma. Some Thanksgiving."

I got up, too. I couldn't see me having a feast at Craddoc's while Robyn was stuck hearing about Grandma's bad back. "I'm calling Craddoc and telling him if he wants to eat at his house it will have to be without me."

Robyn came around the table and dragged on my arm. "No, don't. That will just start a big fight. Give him a month's notice that he's invited to our house for Christmas Eve, and we'll do it all up with popcorn and candy canes."

I gave her a quick hug. "Robyn, you're such a neat sister." Over Robyn's shoulder, I caught Mother watching us with a tender expression I didn't remember seeing before.

In the evening, when I got to Jeanne and Dad's condominium, Teddy, their two-year-old, was stamping up and down, clutching his blanket under his nose, and crying,

"Pea' bu', pea' bu', pea' bu', pea' bu'."

Jeanne had a cup of milk on the kitchen counter and was hurriedly spreading peanut butter on a slice of bread. Teddy grabbed Jeanne's legs and pulled on her nylons. "Pea' bu', pea' bu', pea' bu'."

Jeanne reached down to jerk him loose. "Stop your yowling, Teddy. I'm going as fast as I can."

I picked up Teddy, and he put a sticky hand on each side of my face. "Pea' bu', E'sie?"

"Yes," I told him. "You're going to have a peanut-butter sandwich. Let's get you in your

high chair so you're ready for your dinner."
I tucked Teddy in his seat and tied a bib
around his neck. Jeanne had put off feeding
him until I got there, I knew. If there was
anything Jeanne found tedious, it was poking
food into Teddy.

Jeanne slapped four little sandwiches and
the cup of milk on his tray. "You can give him
a jar of apricots for dessert," she told me.
"There's ham in the refrigerator if you want
to make yourself something."

Teddy's eyes rounded, his sandwich hanging in midair. " 'Am?' 'Am? 'Am?"

"Oh, God!" Jeanne clutched her fingers into
her hair. "*You* take care of him. And could
you please, please baby-sit tomorrow? Ed's
boss is having a brunch at his house and Ed
didn't tell me until yesterday. Maybe you
could stay all night. *Pretty please?*"

"OK," I agreed.

Surprised, Jeanne snapped her mouth
closed. She had been ready to give me a big
sales pitch, not knowing I was delighted to
earn the money for two more Christmas presents before the weekend was over.

There was a pep assembly after second
period Monday and I'd promised to meet
Jenny in the commons so we could go together. I didn't make it. I had just finished
putting the second-semester teaching schedule on the computer when Mr. Olson came in
with his vice-principal face on. "May I see
you in my office, please, Elsie?"

Now what? I followed him with a sinking stomach.

He sat me down across from his desk and started in slowly. "You told me last week that you felt we needed more security around the computer."

Oh, Jee-sus, I should cut my tongue off. "I . . . just thought since grades were out. . . ."

"Well, yes. Do you think you could pick out a tall boy and a short, stocky boy who might be interested in getting at the computer?"

I took a long breath. He'd done it. Rick had done it! "A tall boy and a short, stocky boy? I guess there's lots of those going here."

"Let's say a tall blond boy and a stocky brown-haired boy."

I shrugged and turned up my hands.

"You might think about it some more," he suggested. "Perhaps you'll remember someone who asked you about the computer or someone you heard talking about the passwords. If you come up with anything that would help us, I'd appreciate your letting me know."

I nodded, rose from my chair, and got out of there.

As I walked slowly down the outside corridor toward the gym, I scrinched my shoulders together. Now what was I supposed to do? I didn't really know if it was Rick. Come on, yes I did. Maybe I could suggest to Mr. Olson that he run a new printout of student grades and compare them with those on the backup disks. Ohh, sleazy, Elsie.

Near the gym doors I heard the seniors chanting, "Power! Seniors! Power! Seniors! Power! Seniors!..."

I had to maneuver around the remote-controlled toy car some jerk had following me along the gym floor, trying to entangle my feet. Jenny was sitting halfway up the junior bleachers. I shoved the car away with my foot and climbed up the stands to the seat she was saving for me.

"What kept you?" Jenny asked me.

"Rick must have broken in over the weekend," I whispered, trying to make myself heard over the yelling crowd.

Her eyes widened. "You're kidding. Did he get caught?"

"Not yet."

"How'd you find out?"

"Olson was grilling me about a tall, blond-haired boy and a short, fat boy."

"Oh, oh."

The band struck up the closing number, and while Diane and the rest of the cheerleaders led the singing student body, I read the signs stuck on the gym walls. FAST TIMES AT FIRCREST HIGH ... SENIORS ARE WEEKEND WARRIORS ... WHO'S #*!? YUCKY CAROLINE ... HEY BUD LET'S PARTY.

Craddoc came home on Wednesday, and we went to the football game with Jenny and Einer. Rick Evers ran forty yards for a touchdown. Craddoc shook his head in amazement. "I bet USC takes him."

"What about the U here or Wasu?" Einer asked.

"Naw, I bet he'll go to California," Craddoc said.

After the game we went to Baskin-Robbins to munch down, Einer being about as straight as Craddoc. Jenny had to get up early to help put the turkey in the oven, so Craddoc dropped them off at Jenny's and drove us to our spot overlooking the Sound.

"Nice to be home," he said, pulling me close. "And, ummm, you look good to me."

"Wait a minute. First, I want to ask you a question on morality."

Craddoc raised his eyebrows. "Morality? Elsie, you didn't!"

I shoved against his shoulder. "Now, Craddoc, listen!"

He straightened his back and put his hands on the steering wheel. "OK, I'm ready."

"What if I knew somebody broke into the school and changed their grade on the computer and the vice principal knew I knew?"

"Hmmm." Craddoc scratched his chin. "Did you see the person do it?"

"No, but the person tried to get me to change his grade for him, and when I wouldn't, he got another computer student to help him learn the passwords, and the VP described them to me as the ones who broke in."

"How did the vice principal know you knew?"

"Because before the break-in happened, I

told him to put the electric eye outside the computer room."

"Well, in that case, what choice have you got?"

"It's Rick Evers."

"What?" Craddoc jerked around to face me. "Are you sure?"

"I just told you how sure."

"Start from the beginning and tell me exactly what happened."

So I started from the beginning and told him exactly what happened.

At the end of my tale, Craddoc slumped down in his seat. "Evers wouldn't do it."

"He did it."

"No, he has too much to lose."

"That's what I thought until Olson described him."

"That's not much of a description — tall and blond."

"And short and fat. Who other two?"

Craddoc shook his head. "He'd have too much to lose. He lives with his dad, who's in a wheelchair with multiple sclerosis, and all they've got is his dad's disability pay. Rick has to have a football scholarship. He wouldn't blow it for one grade. That's stupid."

I sighed. "I wonder if they could put an amendment to the ERA outlawing men from clinching their arguments by calling women stupid."

"I didn't call you stupid. I said Rick

wouldn't do anything that stupid. There you go, being defensive again."

"Oh, Craddoc! Let me grow up. I'm not defensive anymore."

Craddoc turned to me with a grin. "Speaking of growing up, I have a little something I want to talk about with you. Have you thought about getting birth-control pills?"

"Not lately."

"Shall we give it a little thought, hmmm? You're going to be seventeen in a couple of weeks." He slipped one hand under my hair at the back of my neck and drew me closer. With the other hand he unbuttoned the top of my coat.

4. The Law of Noninterference

Thanksgiving at Craddoc's house was lavish, as usual. Mrs. Shaw's crystal sparkled, the fat brown turkey glistened, the salad fruit glittered like jewels, and golden butter shimmered on mounds of snowy mashed potatoes. Only one of the grandmothers was there. The other, the one I especially liked, died in the summer. Craddoc sat between an aunt and uncle, and I was surrounded by five of the cousins. The sixth cousin, the aunt explained, was having dinner at his girl friend's house. I narrowed my eyes at Craddoc with that announcement. He looked oblivious, and I stewed to myself about poor Robyn forking into slices of soggy restaurant turkey while listening to Grandma's litany of sleepless nights.

After dinner Mr. Shaw brought out his movie screen, set up the projector, and announced he was going to treat everyone to replays of the WSU football games. I watched the hulking players in their muddy jerseys and caged helmets push each other up and down the playing field until my eyes grew heavy. One of the cousins gave up trying to stay awake and snored softly beside me.

It was easy to tell when Craddoc came into the game, because everything sort of stops for the kicker. He always made the extra point and when he made a field goal the other players hugged him and smacked him on the bottom. His dad had a close-up of Craddoc as he stood on the sidelines after making the only score of a game. Craddoc was watching his teammates move the ball around the middle of the field while the clock ran out, and there was shining pride in his face as he stood confidently with one hand on his slim hip.

The next morning, I lay in my bed trying to decide what I was going to do about Craddoc and sex. Craddoc didn't take "no" well. "No" was hard for me to say, anyway. If you don't make the decision, Elsie, the decision.... It wasn't that I was against it. Craddoc, with his warm brown eyes and thick, broad shoulders.... He must be lifting weights five times a day; even his neck was getting thick. And I don't mean planning ahead made me think I was easy. I didn't think that. It was just that I always thought it would happen when I wanted it so much I couldn't stop myself. Nothing inside me was pushing me to Planned Parenthood, nothing but Craddoc.

Craddoc had to be back at Pullman for a game Saturday afternoon, so if I could just slide out of a confrontation that Friday evening, I'd have until Christmas to make the decision. That thought got me out of bed. As I headed for the bathroom I smelled pancakes. I figured Robyn must be cooking.

I got into the kitchen in time to see a strange boy's face peering in the back-door window. "Who's that?" I asked Robyn.

Robyn turned away from the stove, pancake turner in hand. "Oh, Joe." Her face pinked as she let him in and introduced him to me.

"Hi, Joe," I said.

"Hi," he croaked in his JH voice. "You making something, Robyn?"

"Yes, ooh, they're probably burned!" Robyn hurried to the frying pan, and as she flipped the pancakes over, Joe peered around her shoulder.

"You hungry?" she asked him.

"Sure. I'm on a seefood diet."

"Seafood diet?" she repeated, puzzled.

"Ya, I see it, I eat it."

Robyn giggled and it was like that all the way through breakfast. I escaped when I heard the mailman.

In the fold of the catalogs was a bill from the PUD and a letter from Jack. I dropped the catalogs and light bill on the dining-room table and took Jack's letter into my room to open.

Hello Elsie,

Thanks for writing me back so soon. I liked reading your letter a lot. You know I'm not much for writing letters, but for you, I'll do my best. Moving over here was like moving into a different world. It seems as though your letter is the only connection with the world I came from. Don't get me wrong. I enjoy it here.

Quite a bit has happened to me since I wrote you. I've already got another job. I'm working in the woods now, splitting cedar blocks. Grover changed his mind. I was over at his house with Kevin on a Friday night and we were talking about the woods. I asked him how come he wouldn't let me at least try to split blocks. He looked me up and down, then reached over, squeezed my arm, and said, "Well, maybe a scrawny little kid like you could become a burly cedar rat. Be ready at six o'clock tomorrow morning."

I felt like I was on cloud nine. When Kevin and I got home, Kevin asked me what I was going to use for rain gear. You probably already know, when it rains on the Olympic Peninsula, it rains. I had an old ski jacket and warm-ups, so I told Kevin I'd use those. He thought I was kidding. He had a can of water repellent, which he let me use on the jacket and warm-ups. I used the whole can.

In the morning I went to work with

Grover, and sure enough, it was pouring. Grover showed me how to split the cedar into blocks. Within one hour after he left me to go cut wood, the water repellent had washed off. I was soaked to the bone and freezing. There was no way I was going to let Grover know. Believe me, Elsie, I didn't want him to think I wasn't a good worker, but by the end of the day I felt like I was going to die. On the way home, Grover told me he was impressed with my persistence. He said if I wanted to work, be ready tomorrow at six o'clock.

When I got home, I could not get warm. I went to bed cold and woke up hot. When it came time to get up, I was just too sick. I had a fever, and when I tried to get out of bed, I started coughing. When Grover came over to get me, Kevin told him I was too sick to work. I heard Grover laughing as he left. At that point I felt like crying. I thought I'd blown the job for sure. Then I started worrying that I might lose my mill job, too. So, later on in the afternoon, I called the mill owner and told him I couldn't work Monday morning. He said no problem. Just give him a call when I was ready to go back to work.

You probably think I'm nuts. Why would I want to leave a job in a nice dry mill to work in the wet, cold, slimy woods? More money? I'm making less now than I was in the mill. Glory? No one is around to see me work, not even Grover. He's usually off somewhere cutting more wood with his chain saw. Give up? The mill is boring. It's like working in a factory. My back even got pulled out of place from bending over the same way all day long. Working in the woods is much more interesting. Also, from what I've seen, I'll make more money in the long run, once I get stronger and faster.

It took me about two weeks to get well. A couple days later, Grover came over and asked me if I was ready to go to work. I couldn't believe it. I called the mill owner and told him I was going to work in the woods. Kevin lent me some money to buy some good rain gear, so now here I am. Ya, it seems as though Steve Four-Suns was right. Make your decision, do the best you can to bring it about, and it will work out.

I talked to Steve Four-Suns a little about your problem. He didn't give me a direct answer. I was walking on this trail through the woods near the ocean, when I ran across him sitting on a log. I asked him what he was doing and he said, "Being aware."

I looked where he had been looking, but couldn't see anything in particular to be aware of, so I didn't say anything.

Honestly, Elsie, even though I like Steve, I get a little nervous and shy when I'm around him.

Anyway, after a while, I told him about your incident with Rick at school and asked him what you should do.

He looked over at me and said, "Would you like to go for a walk?"

I told him sure, so we walked up the trail in silence for a ways until we came to a big tree growing in the middle of the trail. It was probably eight feet across, at least. Steve stopped and asked me, "Which way are you going to go around this tree?"

I was standing on the right side of the trail, so I replied, "I was going to go around it to the right."

Steve, still looking at me, said, "What if I wanted you to go around it on the left?"

At this point, I was getting a little nervous, so I asked him why he would want me to do that.

"I might think it better for you to pass the tree on the left. Perhaps if you go around it the other way, you will trip on a root and twist your ankle."

Now I'm thinking to myself Steve might be able to look ahead in time and see that if I walked around the tree like I had planned, I was going to get hurt. So I asked him, "Are you trying to tell me that if I go around this tree on the right I'm going to get hurt?"

Steve replied, "No, all I said was I might think it better for you to pass the tree on the left. Let me ask you this: do you think I should be telling you how to go around this tree?"

When I told him no, he seemed to lighten up a bit. "I agree. I don't have any right whatsoever to tell you where to walk on this trail. I believe nobody has the right to tell another which path to walk upon."

I can't remember everything he said after that, but it had to do with what he called the law of noninterference. After he told me all this stuff, he said he had to go and took off into the woods. He didn't even take the trail. Boy, I'll tell ya that whole scene shook me up. I've been thinking about it for days.

What's amazing me, Elsie, is all of this seems to have happened because of your letter. Thanks again for writing me. Please write again soon.

Have fun,

Jack

P.S. This has to be the longest letter I've ever written.

5. Here's to Snow White

I was reading Jack's letter over when Robyn hollered that Craddoc was there. I found Craddoc in the living room plunking on the piano keys. He wanted to know what I was doing, studying? No, I told him, I got the most interesting letter from Jack, and I started rapping away to Craddoc about the Shaman.

He listened for a moment, then laid a hand on my shoulder to slow me down. "How about telling me the rest in the car? I'm supposed to meet one of the players from Pullman for lunch. Want to go along?"

"I can't. I promised I'd baby-sit Teddy this afternoon so Jeanne can go shopping."

"He's bringing *his* girl."

"No, really, I can't. I promised Jeanne." What would I say to a college girl?

The muscles in Craddoc's jaw tensed the way they do when he's pissed. He put his hands on his hips. "Are you going to be able to break away for my last evening?"

"Naturally. Diane's having a party. Why don't I pick you up at your house about eight-thirty?"

That made him smile a little — my picking *him* up — and he said he'd be sure to be ready on time.

Jeanne was late coming home from shopping, of course. Dad arrived before she did, and I suggested I leave little Teddy with him and split. He didn't go for that, saying he was bushed and needed a shower, so I settled Teddy in front of the TV to watch *Mister Rogers* while I boiled potatoes and carrots. Jeanne arrived just as I was squashing Teddy over the sink to wash the vegetables out of his hair.

"Oh, you've finished feeding him," she said, pleased.

She rounded out the baby-sitting money to fifteen dollars, so I was pleased, too.

There were mass people in Diane's rec room. I spotted Rick Evers leaning over the davenport, grinning down at a glowing Diane. Diane is one of Jenny's friends that I met when we were in the fifth grade. Sharon is another of them, but Sharon joined a youth group a year ago and doesn't go to parties anymore, at least not Diane's parties, which suits me fine because Sharon makes a habit of being the bearer of bad tidings, true or not.

Diane's mother's a widow and doesn't earn as much money as my mother, but she always sees to it that Diane looks great and that all the kids feel welcome in their house. Diane invites me to her parties mostly because of Craddoc, I think, because I'm not part of her cheerleader crowd. Jenny isn't, either, but like I said, they're old friends.

Mixing is easy for Craddoc and we hadn't been at the party five minutes before he got going in a game of pool. I played a couple of turns with him, then wandered off to the refreshment table for some punch. Rick came up and poured himself a half a cup. I guessed he'd finish filling it up out in the garden.

He lifted his cup in a salute to me before he left. "Here's to Snow White."

I wasn't sure just what that meant. Craddoc didn't gossip about private things, I knew. Maybe it was just a crack about my being too pure to break into the computer for him.

I met both Jenny and Diane in the bathroom sometime later. Her face still glowing, Diane was rattling on about what Rick had said to her and what she had said to him. She sighed. "Isn't he a hunk of?"

More like a pile of, I thought to myself.

I got sleepy before Craddoc could even think of leaving. After the second time I asked him if he was about ready to go, I went out into the garden to get some fresh air, hoping it would keep me awake. Larry was out there. He's sort of built like a tractor, but I like him and so does everybody else. I noticed he was putting a round can in his back pocket when I came out. I couldn't see what it was in the dark.

"What have you got?" I asked him.

"Just a little chaw," he mumbled through a full mouth.

"What?"

He shifted the load into his cheek. "Tobacco."

"Isn't that messy?"

"Ya, but I get off on it."

"I thought that was for baseball players."

"And football players. How come you're not in there being a party girl?"

"I don't know how."

"A brain like you?"

"Being a brain doesn't help. I can write it. I can read it. I can figure it out. But when it comes to saying all those little funny things that people like Diane can spiel off, nothing comes out of my mouth. Nothing. Everybody knows the secret but me. All the books say don't think about yourself, talk about what interests the other person. Like what? Anyway, that isn't what Diane talks about or Craddoc talks about."

Larry put his arm around my shoulder and moved us over against an apple tree. "That's OK, Elsie. My mom is just like you. She's smart and she likes to read and she's a fantastic cook, but she'd rather cut off her fingers than join a bridge club. My dad thinks it's just the way she is, and lets her read a book while he goes off to his meetings. If you haven't got a gift of gab, you haven't got a gift of gab. You've got plenty else."

"You're so nice, Larry. No wonder everybody likes you so much."

"But I'm not pretty like Craddoc."

"Big deal."

Larry nodded toward the garden door. "And speaking of Craddoc...."

"What happened to your dying to go home?" Craddoc asked, coming toward us.

"I decided to have my therapy session first." I stood on tiptoes and kissed Larry on the cheek before Craddoc and I left.

"What was that all about?" Craddoc wanted to know as we climbed into my car.

"He was telling me his mother wasn't any better a mixer than I am. He said his dad just lets her be and goes off without her."

"Some marriage," Craddoc said, watching me try to maneuver away from the curb.

The car parked ahead of me and the car behind me had me wedged in so tight I could only inch the MG a half a foot each time I pulled the steering wheel around.

Craddoc opened his door to get out. "Here, let me do it."

"No, I can do it myself."

He closed the passenger door and sat there impatiently until I finally got the car on the road.

"Larry was nice to tell me about his mother," I said.

"But it wouldn't hurt you to try a little harder, would it? You're the only one I know who makes a fuss about meeting new people."

"I'm the only Elsie Edwards," I said, and gunned my car through a yellow light.

We didn't talk the rest of the way to his house. When we got there, he told me his folks were taking him up to Crystal Mountain skiing the first part of Christmas vacation and they were going to Pasadena to the Rose Bowl on New Year's.

"So I won't be seeing you much over vacation," I guessed.

He pulled me close. "Sure you will. Wasu gets out a couple of weeks before the high school does, you know. And . . . uh . . . it will be special this time, right?"

I scrinched my shoulders up toward my ears. "I don't know, I. . . ."

He lifted my chin and kissed me, then traced a finger around my eyes, my mouth. "Elsie, in eight days you'll be seventeen. You're the one I want, but. . . ."

I stiffened. "What does that mean? 'You're the one I want, but'?"

He looked at me thoughtfully. "You want me, too, don't you?"

I put my arms around his shoulders and buried my face in his chest so he couldn't see my eyes.

The next morning, after Robyn and I had cleaned the house and I had typed a five-paragraph theme for English, I drove on over to Jenny's to see what was happening. She and

45

Einer had had a fight, which left her in a foul mood. Kenny, her nine-year-old brother, lugged a pile of old toys out the back door while we were getting Cokes out of the refrigerator. When he came back from the garbage can, Jenny asked him what was going on.

"I'm cleaning out my junk in case Dad and I move to San Francisco."

"You and Dad aren't going to San Francisco alone, dummy."

"Believe anything you want," he answered, shrugging.

Jenny and I went into the living room to finish our Cokes, and after a while her mother came home, made herself some tea, and joined us.

"How's that handsome boyfriend of yours?" she asked me.

"He's all right."

She took a sip of her tea. "You don't sound like he's all right."

"Well, he's giving me a bit of a problem."

"Like what?" Mrs. Sawyer loves to help with other people's problems. I don't mean in a gossipy way like Sharon's mother. You can really trust Mrs. Sawyer.

"Uh . . . like he thinks I should get some pills."

Mrs. Sawyer nodded. "It's that time, eh?"

"Anyway, he thinks it is."

"And you?"

"I don't know. It's just that I always thought I'd be burning all up with desire and could hardly wait. . . . I'm stupid, I guess. Or maybe I'm frigid. I like his kisses and all, but."

Mrs. Sawyer's laughter tinkled in the room. "I think you haven't had the propa' ganda'."

I didn't get it.

"Mother's being cute," Jenny intervened. "She means you don't have the proper gander."

I still didn't get it.

"The right guy," Jenny said flatly.

"It's always seemed like Craddoc's everybody's right guy," I said.

"Not necessarily," Mrs. Sawyer replied.

While I thought that over, Jenny concentrated on interweaving her fingers in her lap, then looked at her mother out of the corner of her eye. "Haven't *you* got the proper gander?"

Mrs. Sawyer's face grew solemn. "I'm not sure that's the right question. I think it's more a matter of am I being allowed to be a person or am I expected to be an appendage."

Jenny appraised her coldly. "You were always the smooth compromiser . . . Mrs. Oil-on-Troubled-Waters."

Her mother raised her eyebrows. "Maybe it's time I developed me."

"Even if it means losing Kenny, not to mention Dad?"

"Even if it means that."

"And if you lose me?"

Her mother looked at Jenny with clear green eyes. "Am I going to lose you?"

"No," Jenny said softly.

It was then that Kenny came into the living room to ask about dinner, so I got up and said it was past time for me to be home.

6. No Problem

Dear Jack,

I got your letter yesterday, unfortunately too late to keep my big mouth shut. I found out that the school has one of those portable electric eyes, and if the beam's broken, it alerts the police. I suggested to Mr. Olson that he put it outside the computer room for the weekend, being as the grades were out and all. Rick must have set the alarm off, all right, but he got away, because Mr. Olson questioned me about knowing a tall, blond boy and a fat, brown-haired boy who would be interested in getting at the computer. I didn't want to lie and I didn't want to say who I thought it was, so I just weasled around, saying nothin. And Rick is still playing football. So much for Goody Two-Shoes or, as Rick calls me, Snow White.

Jenny's been raspy lately and today I

found out why. Her parents may be sepa-
rating. It rocks my head. It always
seemed like Jenny was the lucky one.

Jack, I really don't understand where
the line is between helping and interfer-
ing. I wish there were signposts staked
out in your life saying RIGHT WAY TO GO
and WRONG WAY TO GO. *Then if you*
wanted to do the wrong thing, you'd
know you were doing the wrong thing.
As it is, I feel like a rat in a maze, run-
ning my life by trial and error. And I'm
especially good at hitting the errors. It's
scary.

I stopped writing for a minute. I would
have liked to tell Jack about my problem with
Craddoc, but I thought it might push Jack
away from me. Make things so final. I tried
to figure out why I'd mind that. I couldn't, so
I ended the letter with "Love, Elsie," which I
meant on some level, anyway.

Robyn came into my room while I was re-
reading my letter. She wanted to know what
I thought of Joe. What could I say about a
skinny fourteen-year-old who kept jerking
his head to flip his black hair out of his eyes?

"Seems like he's got a good sense of
humor," I told her.

"Ya," she agreed, smiling happily, "he's so
funny." She sat down on the edge of my bed.
"What are you doing? Writing to Jack?"

"Yes," I said.

"Why don't you ask him what happens to

you if you break the law of noninterference?"

"*Robyn!*"

She slipped off the bed. "You left the letter lying right out."

"That's no excuse. You could have at least asked."

"Anyway," she said at the door, "Jack's letters are a lot more interesting than Craddoc's."

"You wait until you get one from Joe!" I yelled after her.

"He doesn't know how to write!" she shouted back from down the hall. I heard her laughing to herself as her footsteps went toward the kitchen. I hoped she'd cook a decent dinner.

Dinner was OK — sloppy joes, Robyn's specialty. Mother came home when we were halfway through eating. She made herself a drink and sat down at the table.

"You ready to eat?" Robyn asked.

"Not yet," Mother said. "I signed a buyer for that apartment house I've been trying to sell. I hope the deal doesn't flip."

I hoped it didn't, either. If the sale went through, it would mean big Christmas presents from her.

Robyn got up to get our dessert. "Is it all right if I go to a junior-high skating party?"

"How're you going to get there? I'm bushed." Mother did look tired. There were dark circles under her eyes.

Robyn put a slice of gingerbread in front

of me. "Made it myself, Elsie. You can drive me, OK?"

I gave her a look.

"I'll clean the house by myself next Saturday. Then you can go shopping or make some money chasing Teddy around."

I gave her another look.

She smiled down at me. "Pretty please?"

I drove her up to the rink. By the way she wiggled in the seat, I figured Joe was going to be there.

Mother was sitting in the living room doing nothing when I got back. The lamp wasn't turned on beside her.

"I've been waiting until Robyn was gone to ask you a favor," she said.

I sat down on the edge of the davenport, wondering, What?

"Do you have to go to school Monday for anything special?" she asked.

"I don't know. I guess not."

"I mean, do you have a test or anything?"

"No."

"Well, then, could you drive me to the hospital and back?"

I thought a minute. "Why are you going to the hospital?"

"I have to have a biopsy."

"A biopsy for what?" I was leaning forward now, totally alert.

"Probably nothing. I just have this little lump on my chest."

"Your chest?"

She fluttered a hand in the direction of her

left breast. "This side. My breast." She swallowed and kept her face expressionless like she didn't want to show how she felt.

"How long have you had it?"

"I noticed it a couple of weeks ago when I was soaping in the shower. The doctor said maybe it's just a breast cyst. Lots of women get those. He just wants to do a biopsy to be certain it isn't malignant."

"Oh."

"Well, do you think you can drive me?"

"Sure. No problem. What time do you have to be at the hospital?"

"At seven in the morning. Don't let Robyn know, because it's probably nothing. We can tell her I'm going in for an examination."

"All right." I sat there for a minute, uncertain of what to say next. I picked up a copy of *Omni* and leafed through it until the phone rang.

It was Robyn, wanting to be picked up. That was fast.

I saw Robyn huddled under the eaves of the skating rink when I drove up. She hurried into the car. "Jee-sus, it's cold out tonight. Do you think it's going to snow?"

I glanced at the starless sky as I pulled out. "Could be. There's clouds up there. How come you're leaving so early? The skating party isn't over, is it?"

"No."

"Then why'd you leave?"

"You wouldn't understand."

"Try me."

"Joe and Cecile were skating together."

"Wasn't that OK with you?"

"*All* evening?"

"Well, then, why didn't you just skate with someone else?"

Robyn stared out the car window. "I knew you wouldn't understand."

"What's to understand? Joe isn't that big a deal, is he? Just choose another guy."

She turned her head slowly toward me. "Look at yourself. Dimples, big blue eyes, naturally curly hair. You've got a college football hero in love with you, and Jack and Jenny for friends. What do *you* know?"

"It hasn't always been like that, Robyn."

"Ya, you were fat once." She looked out the window again.

"I wasn't just fat. People hated me. Mother took you places, not me."

"What did you want her to do? Roll you down the street beside her?"

I turned the corner toward our house. "You and Mother didn't want me around, and in school every kid in the class hated me."

"What did you expect? You were a thief. I used to hope no one would know you were my sister."

"That was nice of you. You're welcome for the ride." I eased my car next to our curb, turned my lights out, and took the key out of the ignition.

Robyn opened the car door. "You aren't the

only one who's had bad things happen, Elsie Edwards."

We stalked up the front steps and I let the screen door bang in Robyn's face. Mother was still sitting in the living room, but she had a drink beside her now. I tried to make my voice sound pleasant as I said goodnight and went into my bedroom.

7. Guilt Slipping Around My Brain

I set my alarm for five-thirty Monday morning, but Mother was up before me. I drank orange juice and crunched down some whole-wheat toast while she impatiently lit a third cigarette. We didn't talk much in the car on the way to the hospital. Partly because I couldn't think of an appropriate subject, and partly because she was busy folding and unfolding her hands.

In the hospital office, Mother filled out insurance forms, dropping her wallet in her fumbling attempt to get out her Social Security card and Snohomish County Physicians card. We waited in line for the blood tests. When it was Mother's turn, the lab technician had her put her elbow on the lab counter while she tied a small rubber hose around Mother's upper arm. She tapped Mother's vein gently, then slipped a huge hypodermic needle in and drew out a vialful blood.

Up in the hospital room, a nurse had

Mother undress, put on one of those white winged gowns, and get into bed. Mother told me I could leave if I wanted to and come back to pick her up about noon. I stuck around, though, until they took her into surgery.

I didn't have anything special to do before twelve o'clock, so I drove down to Old Mill Town in Edmonds and had a fat cinnamon roll and orange spice tea at Bruseau's. While I was dawdling through a second cup of tea, it hit me. What if Mother *did* have cancer? I took a quick glance down at my own breasts and sucked in my breath. I'd sure hate to lose one.

When I returned to the hospital, a nurse directed me to a large room with beds scattered around in it. Mother was at the far end, sitting on a white-sheeted bed, fully dressed. I hurried across the floor, hoping I wasn't late. "You been waiting long?" I asked her.

"No, but let's get out of here. I need a cigarette."

Down in my car, she lit up her cigarette and inhaled deeply. "Drop me off at the office, will you?" she said.

"Do you feel good enough to work?"

"I'll feel a lot better there than hanging around the house."

"Whatever." I put the car in gear and drove toward her office.

When we were halfway there, she stubbed her cigarette butt into the ashtray, leaned back, and said carefully, "If something should happen to me, I hope you girls will stick together."

"What did the doctor say?"

"Nothing much."

"What did he *say*, though?"

"He said he would get the results of the lab tests on Friday and he would call me then."

"I'd go nuts waiting that long to find out."

We had reached the real-estate office by then. She gathered up her purse and opened the car door. "No doubt I'll be nuts by then, too. Thanks for the ride."

I drove slowly on home, one hand on the steering wheel and the other knuckled against my mouth. What if something *did* happen to her? The last couple of years, I'd mostly just ignored her. I thanked her if she bought me clothes, but I didn't really appreciate her getting them for me. I was too bitter over how she treated me when I was a little kid.

At home, I dumped my books on the kitchen table and worked on a project for my contemporary world problems class until Robyn came in. She nodded to me and I nodded to her. We hadn't been talking much since she'd told me she used to hope nobody knew I was her sister. I *was* gross in those days, and I did steal food and the kids' lunch money to buy candy. It wouldn't even cross my mind to do anything like that now, but the fat me and the skinny me were all me and I didn't appreciate what Robyn had said.

It was her turn to get dinner, so I carried

my junk into my room. I sat at my desk thinking it was strange that Robyn had been home so much lately. She usually went over to Cecile's for a while after school. Maybe the rink party aced her out of Joe and Cecile both. Life of a JH. I shrugged my shoulders and got to work.

Mother *did* go crazy with worry until Friday. When I'd get up in the middle of the night to go to the bathroom, I'd see a light on in the living room and know she was still awake and trying to read. By Thursday I told myself to stop being such a cowardly pig and made myself go in and join her. I sat on the footstool and pulled my nightgown over my knees. "Long wait, huh?"

She looked up from her book and nodded. She started to read again, then put her finger in her place and folded the book partway shut. "Elsie, when your dad and I were divorced, part of the settlement was that he had to start an educational trust fund for you girls. Don't let him ever talk you out of that money by saying he's going to invest it for you so you'll have a lot more."

"Oh, I wouldn't."

"He's a good talker, you know."

"I know."

Mother resumed reading, leaving me to go back to bed. Only now I couldn't get to sleep, with guilt slipping around my brain. What would I do if something happened to her? Robyn and I couldn't both jam into Jeanne and Dad's messy place. And Mother had let us grow up so independently that Jeanne's interference would feel like flies crawling on us.

I wished I'd been a little nicer to Mother. She wasn't much of a mother, but then I'd never been much of a daughter, either, more a pain in the ass. God, I hoped it would just be a cyst.

I was groggy at school on Friday. Mrs. Tabbs was updating some student records on the computer, so I stood around, waiting for her to finish. Because of school laws on confidentiality I wasn't allowed to work on student records, just boring office junk.

When I saw Mrs. Tabbs switching out of the student menu, I asked her, "What happens to a student's grade at the semester if they drop a class after first quarter?"

She looked up at me with her papers in hand. "If the student drops when she's passing, there is no semester grade. If a student drops and she's failing the class, the counselor keeps a record of the failure and the student receives an F at the semester. Why? Are you thinking of dropping a class?"

"No, not right now."

She got ready to leave. "I shouldn't think you'd have to worry about F's."

I smiled at her sweetly as she left the room. Rick was going to be up shit creek at the semester. Or maybe, since football season would be over, his grades wouldn't matter. I wondered if he had enough credits for graduation. As I sat down at the computer with Monday's bulletin, I had an urge to look up his student number. The student lists were in the gray metal slots on the side of the computer desk. My hand was going out for them involuntarily when Mr. Olson opened the door. I hurriedly picked up the bulletin instead.

He held out a sheet of his handwriting. "Will you please let whatever you're doing wait, Elsie, and get me ten copies of this right away? I need these notes for an administrative meeting in fifteen minutes."

I put down the bulletin and took his notes, smiling at him sweetly, too. Whoa, a close one, Elsie.

Mother called while Robyn and I were eating dinner. She asked me to look in her closet and see if her red silk blouse was clean. She couldn't remember if she'd taken it to the cleaners or not. I looked and it was clean. Before I let her hang up, I asked if she'd heard from the doctor. Yes, she had, and it was only a cyst in her breast.

I closed my eyes with relief.

There was no problem, she went on. Well, not exactly no problem. He'd have to watch it in case she got any other lumps.

"How does he do that?" I wondered.

"By taking a mammogram. Listen," she said, "I won't be eating dinner, but I'm coming home to change. Will you and Robyn be there?"

"Robyn might, but I'm going over to Jenny's in a little while." After I hung up I wondered how come she was dressing fancy tonight. She usually went out with her office friends on Friday night wearing whatever she'd been working in.

That little mystery got solved when Mother arrived and introduced Robyn and me to Sam, a big, burly guy who was the broker in her real-estate office.

"Elsie is the solist in the school choir." She had her arm around me while I stood stiffly in her grasp. "We'll have to go hear her in the winter concert."

What was this? She had never been to one of my concerts.

I had my jacket on and was ready to leave when she came into my room to ask me how she looked. She had too much rouge on and too much eye shadow. She must have been trying to cover up the ravages of a week with no sleep. "Your outfit looks great," I said, "but tone down the makeup a little bit. It needs to be more subtle with the color of that blouse."

She peered into the mirror on the back of my door. "I guess you're right. God, I'm getting old."

"No, you're not. You just look a little tired. Why don't you wear your dark blue blouse? It will look good with that gray suit and make your eyes look pretty, and it won't be so noticeable that you're beat."

I waited around until she'd changed, and

then told her she looked great. She did look better. Mother and Sam and I all walked out to our cars together, leaving Robyn alone in the house.

When I pulled up at Jenny's, there was a big white FOR SALE sign stuck in her front yard. "What's with the sign?" I asked her at the door.

She grimaced. "We're moving."

"How come?"

Kenny was on the floor in the living room reading the funnies, and Jenny pointed her head toward her bedroom.

Following her in, I felt cold apprehension in my stomach. Without Jenny, I would be as lonesome as Robyn was without Cecile. I hadn't even said good-bye to Robyn, not that she deserved it.

Jenny turned her stereo on and we settled back on the pillows on her bed. Her room is flowery and flouncy, with ruffled curtains, ruffled bedspread, and pom-poms stuck in her dressing-table mirror. I have a fat down quilt that I love covering my bed, and two book-cases crammed with books on each side of my desk. Different personalities and different rooms, I guess.

Jenny picked up her cat from the bottom of the bed and curled it against her chest. "They've done it."

"What?" I asked cautiously.

"Decided to separate."

"You're kidding!" I couldn't believe it.

Jenny had the perfect parents, the perfect family. "How come?"

"Well, as my mother explained it to me, they've reached an impasse."

I propped myself up on my elbow to look at Jenny's face. "Like what?"

"Like my dad's company has offered him a better position in San Francisco. Naturally, he wants to take it. My mother has her position here as manager of EverBloom nursery and she doesn't want to leave her job after all the work she's put into it and the big success she's had expanding the place. So."

"What are you going to do?"

"Stay with Mom, I guess. At least until I graduate."

"What about Kenny?"

"He'll go with Dad."

"Your mother's giving up Kenny?"

Jenny stared at the ceiling while she stroked the cat's gray fur. "I guess so."

"I can't believe it. Your mother'd give up Kenny for a job?"

"The way she puts it is that that's no different than Dad giving up me for a promotion." Jenny dropped the cat over the edge of the bed and got up to change the record. I figured she'd put on a sad song and she did.

8. You're a Big Girl Now

Saturday afternoon I was waiting around for the mail to come when the phone rang. It was Jeanne. She wanted me to come over after dinner. I thought the request was strange since it was my birthday, but maybe she didn't know.

"I'm not exactly sure what I'll be doing tonight," I hedged.

"Well, come for an hour, OK?" she asked.

I agreed, for an hour. I couldn't imagine what she could do in that short time and I was wary because Jeanne's hours can stretch like rubber bands. Birthdays make me nervous, anyway. I never know if anybody'll remember. Once, when I was eleven, Mother completely forgot.

While I was talking to Jeanne, I saw Robyn go to the door for the mail, drop some of it on the dining-room table, and take the rest to her room. I picked up the pile she had left behind. All catalogs. Not even a birthday card from Craddoc or Jack. Wa-ait a minute.

I jerked open Robyn's bedroom door. She was standing by her desk and whirled around to face me. I looked her straight in the eyes. "Are you reading my mail again?"

"What mail?"

"Any of my mail."

"Just because I read one Jack's letters which you left lying out —"

"And Craddoc's letters, which I did not leave lying out."

She stretched out both her hands. "I haven't been reading your mail. Honest."

"It certainly is strange that I didn't get a card from either Craddoc or Jack today."

She stared at me silently.

I waited a few minutes and then slammed out her door.

In the living room I gathered up the catalogs and sat down on the davenport to read them. If you ever buy anything out of a catalog, you not only get catalogs from that company for the rest of your life, but ones from fifty other companies, too. They must make half their money selling consumer lists to each other.

I was leafing through the Wear-Guard advertisements of work clothes when I stopped abruptly at a picture of knee-high rubber boots with steel toes. Perfect for Jack in the rain forest. $22.99. Plus shipping, of course. I was getting up to count the money in my purse when there was a tap on the door and Jenny came in with a birthday present.

I sat back down on the davenport and she

crowded in close to me while I carefully
slipped off the ribbons and pulled away the
Scotch tape. Jenny and her mother make such
pretty packages that I always like to save the
wrappings.

"Hurry up," she told me. "Mom is waiting
outside."

"How come?"

She grimaced. "We have to go look at con-
dominiums."

I'd hate to live in a condo. I'd feel like I was
living in a beehive. But I didn't say that to
her. I said, "I hope you get one in the Fircrest
area."

"We will. I am *not* changing schools. Well,
do you like it?"

I was holding up the multicolored shawl
she had given me. "It's gorgeous. I love the
colors."

Robyn had come into the room by then.
"You're supposed to wear it over one
shoulder," she said.

"I know that," I told her shortly. I draped
the shawl over me and strutted around the
room.

"It's all wool," Jenny said. "Luckily I
found it on sale at Frederick's or I never
could have afforded it. I figured the lavenders
and blues will go with about everything
you've got."

I looked down at myself. "Even my jeans."

Robyn was watching me with her hand on
one of the dining-room chairs. "You're not
supposed to wear it with jeans."

"I *know*!"

She disappeared into the kitchen.

There were a couple of sharp honks from outdoors and Jenny stood up. "Mom's getting impatient. Have a happy birthday. I gotta go." She flew out the door just as the phone rang again.

It was Mother asking me and Robyn to meet her at The Crazy Lobster at six o'clock. Sam was taking us all out to dinner. I didn't say anything for a minute. "For your birthday celebration," she added.

"I hardly know Sam," I said.

"That's all right. He wants to take you."

That was a bit hard to believe, but whatever.

I waited impatiently in my car for Robyn. I was about ready to start up without her when she came out the door loaded with packages. She put them on the ground outside the car while she climbed in and then reached out the door and stacked them on her lap.

As I poked the key in the ignition I spotted an envelope with Jack's writing on it on top of the boxes she was holding. "What's that?"

"I didn't open it. Really, Elsie. I was just saving everything for your birthday dinner. For a surprise." She looked like she was going to cry.

I thought that over while I started up the car.

Mother and Sam were waiting for us in the restaurant lobby. Sam herded us to a table overlooking the ferry dock and waved away the menu cards the waiter was trying to pass around. "Let's all have lobster with drawn butter and Dungeness crab cocktails How about it?"

Mother beamed. "The apartment sale went through today."

"Aw right!" I said. "It's going to be a merry Christmas."

Sam gave Mother's shoulder a squeeze. "More than just a merry one."

Oh, oh.

"Why don't you open some of your presents while we're waiting for the cocktails?" Mother suggested.

I picked up the biggest one from the pile Robyn had placed on the floor beside my chair. It was funnel-shaped. I couldn't imagine what it was. Robyn watched me intently as I opened the card attached to the package. The outside of the card showed two girls holding hands. The taller girl's hair had been color-crayoned into yellow curls. Inside was printed: TO THE BESTEST SISTER IN THE WORLD. Below the "Love, Robyn" were some words written in tiny script: "I'm sorry I said those mean things and made you feel bad."

I looked up and saw her eyes were swimming with tears. "Open the present," she said quickly.

The present was a wastebasket made of two thin metal circles with walnut wood strips woven in between. "It's handsome," I said. And it was.

Sam took it from my hands. "An excellent job. Did you make it, Robyn?"

"I made it in shop. I thought Elsie needed something better than a Baskin-Robbins ice-cream container for a wastebasket.

That did it. I got up and hugged her while she averted her head so no one could see her face crumple. Mother looked at us questioningly before I sat down. Fortunately, the cocktails were served.

I opened the rest of the presents while we waited for dessert. Mother gave me a car stereo. Wow. Sam said he'd install it for me. Craddoc sent me a book of American folk songs, 1770 to 1970.

"Are Woody Guthrie's songs in there?" Mother's always had a crush on Arlo Guthrie and his white Mercedes convertible.

I looked through the 1930s index. "Three of them."

"Good." She smiled.

I read on through the 1960s index. "There's even 'Alice's Restaurant.' "

She reached out her hands. "Let me see."

I gave her the book and opened Craddoc's card. The card had originally said: HAPPY BIRTHDAY 7-YEAR-OLD. Only Craddoc had penned a 1 before the 7. On the outside he'd written: "Remember! You're a *big* girl now." I didn't want to think about that.

Before I could get to Jack's card, the chocolate mud pies arrived. Mine had a lighted candle stuck in it. The waiter was young and good lookin and he gave me a sly smile as he placed the dessert in front of me.

Mother hesitated before she picked up her spoon. "If I keep eating this stuff, I'll be fat as a pig."

"Fine," Sam said. "A man likes something he can sink his fingers into."

After I'd scraped up the last of the fudge from my dish, I tore open Jack's envelope. There was a letter and a card. The letter started out: "Happy Birthday, Elsie! Before you read any further open the card." So I did. Inside was a gold chain. Robyn came around the table and helped me clasp it on my neck.

"Who's this Jack?" Sam asked. "I thought the big boy was the kicker."

"He is," I said. "Jack's just a friend."

"That so?" Sam added up the check in his head and pulled some bills from his wallet for the tip. "Well, how about a movie for the birthday girl?"

I folded Jack's letter into the envelope to read later. "I'm sorry. I'd like to, but I can't. I have to baby-sit. Thanks for the lovely dinner, though. Mother hardly ever buys us lobster."

"I guess not!" Mother laughed. I'd never seen her look so happy.

Robyn rode back with me. "Do you think it's serious between Mother and Sam?" she wondered.

"Who knows?" I paused at the Main Street light. "Shall I drop you off at home?"

"Might as well. I haven't got anything else to do."

She looked so forlorn, slunk down in the car seat, that I told her again how great I thought her present was and offered to take her along with me.

"You sure I won't be in the way?"

"Oh, come on. It's your dad's place. How come you never do anything with Cecile anymore?"

"She's busy with Joe."

"What does Cecile's mother think of that?"

"She doesn't like him, but she can't very well refuse to let him in the house. Cecile was fourteen last month."

"I guess you'll have to branch out and get some new friends, then."

"Sure. Do you know any girls my age who live within ten blocks? I haven't got a car, you know. What would you do if Jenny moved away?"

So much for sisterly advice.

Jeanne and Dad's was a surprise. They were sitting around the living room waiting for me with a big cake and huge present on the coffee table. I had to go through the blowing out of candles and slicing the first piece, trying to ignore the fact that I was stuffed.

After Teddy had smeared frosting all over himself, he dragged on my skirt. "Op' pres', op' pres', op' pres'."

I "op'ed pres'" for fifteen minutes while Teddy hopped up and down and Jeanne and Dad looked pleased with themselves. When I had three yards of tissue paper unraveled on the floor, I came to a blue leather wallet.

"I can sure use a new one of these," I said, thanking them.

"You better check inside and see if it's OK." Dad had a wide smile on his face.

I looked over the credit-card section, tried the clasp on the coin purse, and then pulled open the paper-money slot. A bill. Fifty dollars. "Fifty dollars!!"

Robyn grabbed it. "Let me see. I've never had a fifty-dollar bill."

I grabbed it back. "Well, neither have I."

I thanked Jeanne and Dad and then thanked them again.

"Ah, well," Dad said. "You're a pretty little seventeen-year-old."

"And you're a pretty good baby-sitter, too," Jeanne added. "I hope you're going to sit for me again this summer."

I hoped I wasn't. I wanted a better job, but this was no time to talk about that.

On the way home, I told Robyn that now I'd be able to buy Jack a pair of boots to keep his feet dry in the woods.

She raised her eyebrows. "What are you getting Craddoc?"

"I haven't figured that out yet," I said.

9. Seventeen Changes

Before I went to sleep, I turned on the book light above my bed and read Jack's letter.

Happy Birthday, Elsie!

Before you read any further open the card.

I'm on my feet money-wise now. It sure feels good. I was up in Forks the other day, so I bought you this chain for your birthday. I decided gold would look best on you. I hope you like it.

Your letter was the bright spot in my day. It was really nice to come home after a hard day's work and find it waiting for me.

It sounds like things are really cooking around Fircrest. I never thought they would be installing electric eyes. Do you want to know what's been happening here?

Since there is only one bedroom in the house, I'm sleeping on the couch in the living room. Lisa's baby, Gwenivere, sleeps on the floor in a corner of the room. I was beginning to think there was something wrong with Gwenivere because she never cried.

Gwenivere caught a cold recently and has been coughing a lot. Last night I woke up to her coughing. She coughed a bit, started gasping, then silence. . . . I sat up, but I couldn't hear her breathing. All of these visions were bouncing around in my head. The baby dying while I lay there peacefully sleeping. Lisa having a heart attack when she discovered her baby dead in the morning.

I didn't have any clothes on, but I got off the couch anyway in order to listen better. I still couldn't hear her breathing. I walked over to where she was sleeping. Still silence. . . . I thought, "Oh, my God, if she's dead, what then?"

I leaned over her. Still silence. I stuck my ear right next to her mouth while bending over her. Still silence! Suddenly, she opened her eyes real wide, took one look at my face about an inch from hers, and started screaming.

I stood up totally stunned. Lisa burst out of the bedroom. It looked pretty bad. Me standing over her baby stark naked with the baby howling.

"What have you done to Gwenivere?" Lisa looked at me like I was a pervert molesting her daughter.

I tried to explain to her how I thought Gwenivere had stopped breathing. She definitely didn't buy my story even though it was the truth. Kevin had come out of the bedroom and was trying to figure out what was going on as Lisa picked up Gwenivere and headed back in. In the shuffle, I snuck back to the couch with its covers.

It took me some time to get to sleep after that because Gwenivere wouldn't stop crying. Now every time I get near that baby she starts screaming. Guess she knew how to cry after all.

With my heart I wish you the best birthday,

Jack

I let the pages of the letter fall on my quilt while I laughed over Jack's description of Lisa's baby. Then a strange feeling came over me thinking about Jack standing there naked. I wondered what he looked like. The thing is, being raised in a family of three females, you don't know much about how males really look. The drawings in the health book aren't that good. I turned out my light and fell asleep wondering. Was Jack's hair red like on his head?

There was so much going on the next few days I didn't get a chance to write Jack back until Thursday evening. I shut my door, settled down at my desk, and began.

Dear Jack,

So many things have happened lately I don't know where to start. First off, I feel like I'm changing or growing or coming together or something. And it sounds like you are, too. The working part, I mean. I see you can still get yourself in trouble.

The changing me is kind of hard to explain. I feel a power over people I never felt before. Like I do matter. For so many years I knew I was nothin or worse than nothin. Now power is tilting my head. It started with my getting pissed off at Robyn for saying it was no big thing that I was fat once and then telling me that when I was, she had hoped no one knew I was her sister.

She laid this on me after she'd lost her first boyfriend to her best friend Cecile, and Cecile to her boyfriend. She was feeling lousy, I guess, and took it out on me. After that I shut her down. She got sadder and sadder and on my birthday could barely keep from crying. I gave in and hugged her when she gave me a walnut wastebasket she'd made in shop. Not because of the present, but because it got to me that she was trying so hard.

The next morning, on Sunday, Mother's new boyfriend, Sam, was over and Robyn and I were harmonizing on "Bye-Bye Blackbird" as we did the breakfast dishes. I went out into the living room after we were finished and heard Sam tell Mother he thought I had exceptional talent. When Mother saw me, she said in a new, sugary voice, "When is your school's winter concert, Elsie?"

Her manner irritated me. "What difference does it make?" I asked her. "You never go, anyway."

Before I walked out of the living room I saw Mother look three ways while Sam stared at her with a solemn, appraising expression on his face.

Power.

Then Jenny's folks are splitting because her dad has a promotion if he'll go to SF, and her mom won't move because of her job here. Impasse, Jenny says her mom calls it.

At first, Jenny seemed to take it all right. Then last Saturday her house was sold and her mother signed the papers on a new condominium and Kenny and his dad are leaving Saturday and Jenny asked me to help her pack her things this weekend. The finality of the whole thing hit her, I guess, and she's looking pale and clinging to me, wanting to know if I can't stay all night Friday, too. I think the worst part for her is losing her little brother.

Then — this is turning into a soap

opera — I almost got caught poking into Rick Evers' business again. He'll get an F at the semester in the class he erased (or I think he erased) on the computer at the quarter. I was dying to see if he had enough credits to graduate without it or if he'd have to change the computer again. Luckily, Mr. Olson came in before I tapped into the student menu. I don't know about the law of noninterference, but interference definitely has its pitfalls.

And then — do you remember a Tessie Jones? A sort of pretty sleaze? Rick calls her a stinking animal because she sleeps with everybody . . . anybody? Well, we have a tutoring system in math class where the A students tutor the C and D students before each test. I always get chosen first as a tutor and the other slow students moan when the first one requests me. Power? Flattery?

The math teacher asked me after school Monday if I'd consider tutoring in the special ed classes. For a credit every ninety hours. I said I didn't really need the credit (I'll have more than enough to graduate next year) and anyway I already had a TA with Olson on the computer.

She said I could do the tutoring after school and extra credits should be fine for me because she thought I'd probably be bored in my senior year and had I thought of graduating at midterm and starting college early? Hmm. That sounded good. Only two semesters more of school. So she sent me over to the special ed section (it's in the back half of the history unit) to talk to one of the teachers there. Guess who's my first pupil? Tessie Jones!

While I was leaving the special ed department after my interview, guess who I met in the hall? Bad Helen. Remember her in sixth grade? We used to call her "Hell" and she was the worst kid in the school (even worse than me in fifth grade) and she couldn't read? I guess she still has trouble reading because she said she comes into the special ed classes for history and English. She seemed poised about it, matter-of-fact. She still has her Liza Minnelli haircut and is something to look at. When I first saw her, I stuttered around, "Hi, Hell . . . uh . . . uh . . . Helen." She laughed.

What I'm trying to say, Jack, is I feel the whole reality of me is shifting. Or maybe my reality of me. From a frightened blob to?? I could make Mother scared of me now. I wouldn't do it. I won't do it — I don't think. But there is something in me that would like a bit of tit for tat. I think that's the part of myself I better erase. I was almost too mean to Robyn.

Can you make any sense of this letter?
I hope you come home for Christmas.
I miss you,
Elsie
Oh, oh! I loved the gold necklace. I only
take it off when I go to bed.

When I finished Jack's letter, I wrote Craddoc, too, and thanked him for the songbook. I didn't say anything about remembering I was a "big girl" or tell him that I had driven by the Planned Parenthood office Wednesday afternoon but couldn't make myself go in.

10. I Don't Know Anything

Mother came into my room Friday morning while I was dressing for school. "That's pretty," she said, watching me drape the shawl over my lavender turtleneck. "Where'd you get it?"

"Jenny gave it to me for my birthday." I walked past her to get my raincoat out of my closet.

"When's your winter concert?"

"In a couple of weeks. I'm going to stay over at Jenny's tonight so I can help her pack tomorrow."

"They sold their house?"

"Yes." I stood in front of Mother with my books in one hand and my overnight bag in the other, waiting for her to move so I could go out the door.

"I wish you'd told me when they were going to put the house up for sale."

"I thought you were specializing in business properties now."

She shrugged, making no move to get out

of the way. "I can always use another listing."

"Hmm, well, I gotta go."

She put her hand on the knob but didn't open the door. "What date is your winter concert?"

"It's no big deal," I said impatiently.

"You're going to solo, aren't you?"

"I soloed when I was in the seventh grade."

She opened the door a little bit. "I've never seen you."

"I know."

"Sam would like to hear you."

"Mother, I'll be late for school. What are you doing, selling Sam a package deal? Am I the drapes or the rug?"

She reddened. "I don't see why you're being so evasive about having us in the audience."

"Because you're five years too late."

"Well, real-estate work is all hours."

"You weren't working five years ago. That's before Dad got married and reduced the support payments. Now, I've got to go." I walked around her and pulled on the edge of the door so she had to back up.

"Elsie, it's embarassing me not to even know when you're going to sing."

"*Embarrassing*! Try being the only kid in choir, year after year, whose mother isn't in the audience."

Outside, I rammed my car into gear and roared over to Jenny's house, bitter memories pounding in my head.

Jenny was waiting on the curb. "What kept you?"

"My mother. She wants to impress her new boyfriend with a loving little family."

"How?"

"By taking him to my winter concert."

"Oh." Jenny looked around the inside of my car as I started it up. "Aren't you going to stay all night with me?"

"My bag's behind the seat. Only I have to tutor for a half hour after school."

"That's OK. I can study in the library."

She had to wait longer than a half hour while I tried to get the relationship betwen decimals and percents through Tessie Jones's head.

"Listen, Tessie," I said, "imagine a whole orange."

She gave me a deadpan stare.

"OK, listen." I took off my shawl and hung it over the teacher's chair beside the blackboard. I was beginning to sweat. "I know this sounds like first grade, but just go along with me, OK?" I drew a circle on the blackboard. "Imagine this is a whole orange. *One*, got it?"

"Got it," she said.

"Now you can write one" — I wrote down a 1 on the blackboard — "or you can write one followed by a decimal point, or one with a decimal point after it and two or more zeros. It all equals one. Just one orange." I looked into her green eyes. I couldn't tell if I was getting anywhere or not. "Now, if we change from oranges to dollars, one dollar equals one whole dollar, and we write it one, point, zero, zero. Right? One half a dollar, or fifty cents, we write point, five, zero. Right?"

I glanced up from my numbers on the board. It seemed a glimmer of understanding was coming through. "Fifty percent of one dollar, one half of a dollar, and fifty cents are all the same amount. Follow me so far?"

Tessie nodded.

"Now, you can convert decimals to percents and percents to decimals very easily...." And on and on. By four o'clock I had Tessie saying twenty-five percent of an orange, one fourth of an orange, twenty-five hundredths of an orange. I dropped the chalk in the tray. "Do you live around here?"

She took her jacket off a chair and put it on. "I live in Mountlake Terrace. I can hitch a ride."

I picked up my raincoat, shawl, and books, and we walked out of the unit together. Jenny was waiting outside.

"What happened to the library?" I asked her.

"The librarian wanted to go home."

On the drive to her house, Jenny cranked up my new stereo. "Your mother must have put out some bucks for this. Who installed it?"

"Sam did, Sunday."

"Sam?"

"Her new boyfriend. You know," I said, waiting for the light at Aurora Village to turn, "teaching Tessie is like slogging through glue."

Jenny changed channels to avoid a screeching commercial on rental furniture. "I sympathize with her."

"It's not the same with you. You psyched yourself out of math when you stumbled over fractions in the fifth grade."

"That's what I did?"

We drove past Aurora Village, and seeing Frederick's big white building reminded me that I still didn't have a present for Craddoc. "Do you think Craddoc would like a wallet for Christmas?"

"Sure," Jenny said. "Especially with fifty dollars in it."

"Really. Anyway, the way Tessie stares at me makes me feel like she knows more than I do about things but is too stricken or something to say anything. She tries to get abstractions, but it's like something muffles her brain."

"Elsie, I'm sorry, dear, but you're not making sense," Jenny said in her mother's voice. "And besides, a cop is behind us."

I put both hands on the wheel, paid attention to my driving all the way to Jenny's curb, and let out a sigh when the officer pulled around us.

Dinner at Jenny's was strange. We had hot dogs and bean soup because we were eating the dregs from the freezer. Mrs. Sawyer chattered about nothing, two red spots glowing hotly on her cheeks. Kenny pretended he enjoyed his hot dog, but I noticed he had trouble swallowing each bite. Before we got to the melting ice cream, he rose from his chair. "Well, guess I'm full. I better pack up my junk."

Breakfast was even stranger. The milk was warm from the defrosting refrigerator. Kenny took just one gulp. "Well, Dad, I'm ready. Shall we hit the road?"

Mr. Sawyer took a last sip of coffee, the only thing he'd touched. "Yep, let's get the stuff in the car."

Jenny's mom messed with the scrambled eggs on her plate a bit longer, then gave up to watch out the living room window. Jenny and I followed her. When Kenny and his dad had everything loaded, they came in to say good-bye.

Mr. Sawyer kissed Jenny and told her to be a good girl. Jenny tried to laugh through her tears. He took Mrs. Sawyer's hand. "I'll call you when we get a phone in and give you the number so if you need anything. . . ."

"I'm sure we'll be fine," Mrs. Sawyer said.

Kenny stepped forward and held out his hand. His mother took it solemnly, biting her lower lip to stop its trembling.

"'Bye, Mom," he said. "'Bye, Sis."

Jenny grabbed him, hugged him tight, and tousled his hair. When she released him, Kenny nodded to me, his brown eyes huge in his stark white face, and walked stiffly out the door.

We watched him wave after he got into the car. Mrs. Sawyer gave a feeble wave back with the tips of her fingers, and as the car slipped out of sight, her head sagged onto the windowpane, tears streaming down her face.

"So that's the end of my little brother," Jenny said to her. "I hope you know what you're doing."

Mrs. Sawyer moved her head back and forth against the pane. "I don't know anything for sure."

Jenny and I did up the breakfast dishes and packed them into one of the boxes littering the kitchen floor. Everything was labeled: KITCHEN, LINEN CLOSET, JENNY'S BEDROOM.

"You get your own room in the condominium?"

"Yes," Jenny said. "You'll see."

But I didn't stay to see. Einer, Rick Evers, and Diane drove up in a U-Drive truck to begin the moving and I felt out of place.

Diane started an introduction. "You know Rick, don't you?"

I nodded that I knew him and Rick nodded back.

Rick and Einer tilted the freezer onto a dolly and pushed it out the door. Diane looked after Rick with a blissful expression. "Rick's so strong, isn't he?"

"Einer's no wimp." It was true. Einer's a big-boned Scandinavian, but I had spoken too sharply. I knew I'd better get out of there.

Jenny walked me to the door. "Thanks a lot

for staying with me. I know it wasn't fun for you, but it made it easier for me."

"Oh, it was nothing, old friend," I said, and caught myself before I tousled her hair.

Driving home, I switched the windshield wipers to Fast. The December rain was thickening into sleet. No money for snow tires. Pu-lease don't snow until after Christmas. Sleet and thinking of a concert without Kenny in the audience beaming at his "star" were depressing. I wished I'd gone into his room and sat on his bed and talked to him while he was packing his "junk."

Robyn and I started dinner before Mother got home. "Now don't get mad at me," Robyn said, "but I told Mother the date of your winter concert."

I kept eating my pear-and-cottage-cheese salad.

"You're not mad, are you?"

"No, it's no big deal either way. It just pisses me off that she only comes when she can show off to Sam."

"Elsie, you ... I don't want you mad at me again."

"I'm not going to get mad at you, Robyn."

"Well, when you get mad at someone you stay mad for an awfully long time."

"Robyn!"

"OK, OK, I'll get off it, but Mother isn't the wicked witch.

"Not if you're her little darling."

Mother came in about that time, and

Robyn served her dinner. It was my turn to do dishes, so I started rinsing them for the dishwasher.

After she finished eating, Mother stayed at the table sipping her coffee and flicking ashes off her cigarette into the ashtray. "Elsie," she asked me quietly, "is it all right with you if Sam and Robyn and I come to your concert?"

"What?" It was hard to hear her over the water running in the sink.

She turned around to face me. "Do you object to my going to your winter concert?"

"Whatever."

"I'd appreciate it if you'd come and sit down with me so we could talk."

I dropped the wet paper towel I was wiping the counter with, turned off the water, and came over and pulled out a chair. "I've noticed," I said, "whenever Craddoc says we are going to have a little talk, it's about improving me, not him."

"I know I've made a lot of mistakes with you." She concentrated on putting out her cigarette. "It's funny. We're mother and daughter and I don't even know how to begin this conversation."

"Maybe that's because you haven't had much practice talking to me."

"Elsie, a lot of it is that you remind me of myself. And I guess I mix us up and treat you the way my mother treated me."

"I am not you."

"I know, but. When you're feeling bad. . . .

The mess with your father and my finding out about his other women made me unhappy for a long time, and when you're unhappy you don't act very well. Do you understand?"

"Perfectly," I said icily. "How come you didn't understand when I stole food because I was unhappy?"

Her arms were resting on the table and she turned her palms up in a gesture of hopelessness. "I can't do over the past. I'm sorry about how I treated you but I can't undo it. I've tried hard the last couple of years to be careful not to take my frustrations out on you again."

"Because two years ago I said I'd live with Dad if you didn't back off."

"It wasn't because you said you'd live with Ed that made me try to change. It was because I felt you hated me." She sat staring down at her outstretched hands.

"Come to the concert if you like," I said, getting up. "I'll be nice in front of Sam."

"That wasn't why —" She lifted her head and I noticed for the first time that the edges of her mouth turned down sadly when she wasn't smiling, the same as mine did.

11. Waiting for Seventeen

The Fircrest winter concert was held on Tuesday night, the day before school let out for vacation. Mr. Krakowski and I had our only argument in three years over the program. He announced at our first rehearsal that we would begin the program with "Deck the Halls," followed by "The Twelve Days of Christmas."

"Not 'The Twelve Days of Christmas'!" I moaned. "That song drags so, every kid in the audience is squirming before the sixth day."

"I'm ready to puke on the first partridge," Dave, the piano player, said.

"Now, come on." Mr. Krakowski continued handing out the carol folders. " 'The Twelve Days' is a traditional Christmas song."

"That doesn't keep it from being boring," I insisted.

"She's right," Dave said. "It sucks."

Mr. Krakowski put the remaining folders down on the stands and placed his hands on his hips. "All right, Elsie. All right. I'll make you a trade. You can sing any song you wish, all by yourself, as long as I get to direct the rest of the program."

"Take him up on it, Elsie," Dave told me. "We'll stun 'em."

"And you rehearse on your own time," Mr. Krakowski added.

"You're on," Dave said.

"OK," I agreed.

So the Neophonics rehearsed the endless "Twelve Days" and Dave and I met after school on Tuesdays and Thursdays when I didn't tutor Tessie. Dave's a short, fat-bottomed boy who usually is swinging the top of his body back and forth to the music he hears in his head. I wanted to sing "I Heard the Bells on Christmas Day" as a sort of relevant statement against the armor rattling up and down our continent, and Dave agreed.

He thought we should start out the song with the sound of church chimes, and I agreed. The problem was, chimes or bells were easy but *church* bells were not. Luckily, his father had gone to the University of Washington when the chimes were played on the top of Denny Hall and he remembered the sound of carols ringing across the campus. Dave made a trip to the U music department and got help ferreting out an old recording of the chimes being played the days before Christmas. We were on.

Mr. Krakowski was tactful enough not to assign me a part in "The Twelve Days of

Christmas," but he had me begin "Silent Night, Holy Night" with a gentle solo that hushed the audience. The rest of the choir joined me on the second verse and we ended to loud applause. I spotted Jenny and Robyn beating their hands, and my mother beaming beside Sam.

I'm not usually nervous at concerts. The ham in me takes over and I smile and bow with aplomb. But when Mr. Krakowski announced that the next item on the program was a student production by Elsie Edwards and Dave Johnson, I felt a sharp catch in my stomach. I stepped forward from the soprano section, hoping I wouldn't trip onto my face.

Dave began the bells softly, increased the volume until the old carols filled the auditorium, and then gradually faded them away. I opened my mouth, and my voice came out clear and true as I sang, unaccompanied, "I heard the bells on Christmas day, their old familiar carols play. . . ."

When I came to "And in despair I bowed my head. There is no peace on earth, I said," Dave let the chimes drift into the background, rise in volume for a few seconds after I finished, and slowly drift off.

Total silence.

Then a burst of applause so loud it deafened my ears. One by one the people stood; I saw my mother in tears, and a loud "Bravo!" came from the back of the audience. It was Craddoc! I bowed and bowed and stretched my hand out to Dave, who bowed. While the audience still stood clapping, I moved back to my place in the stands and Mr. Krakowski took over the microphone. "I think we have a little talent there."

The audience laughed and gradually took their seats.

After the last chorus of "I Wish You a Merry Christmas" was sung, the concert was over and we marched off the stands. I was in the back room taking off my red scarf and white robe when I was grabbed from behind. I whirled around into Craddoc's arms.

"Oh, Craddoc!" I hugged him. "When did you get in town? I saw you from the stage."

"You mean you heard him from the stage," Dave corrected me.

"That, too." Craddoc laughed. "I got in late last night. I tried to phone you early this evening, but there wasn't any answer. So I called around a bit until I pinned you down here."

"Mother's got a new friend and he took us out to dinner." I hung my robe on the pole by the side wall. Kids kept congratulating me and I kept telling them it was my sound man Dave who pulled it off, which it was.

Craddoc took me by the arm. "Come on. I've got a car outside. Let's get going."

"What's this? You're dragging me away early? You're the one who hangs around until the birdies sing."

"The birdies have already sung and this is *our* night."

Oh, oh. Apprehension slipped through me.

I didn't think this night was going to turn out quite as Craddoc thought.

He steered me as quickly as he could through the crush in the auditorium. Thank you, thank you, I kept nodding to the complimenters. Jenny, her mother, and Einer stopped us halfway across the floor. Mrs. Sawyer kissed me. "This was your night, love."

My mother stood behind her, awkward and misty-eyed. Robyn edged around, followed by Cecile. "Well, Cecile," I said, "long time no see."

Cecile made a face. "I got dumped, too."

"You better form a girls' support group," I advised them.

"No," Robyn said. "We're going to form a Mafia. I'm going to be the Godmother and Cecile's going to be the hit-person."

Tessie Jones shyly touched my arm, told me how wonderful I had sounded, and introduced me to her dumpy mother, who smiled through a broken tooth, exhaling fumes of alcohol. I moved back to include Craddoc in the introductions, which turned out to be unnecessary. Tessie underwent a subtle change as she greeted Craddoc with half-lidded eyes. "Hello, Craddoc," she said, no longer shy.

"Hi, Tessie," Craddoc answered, grinning. What?

Sam moved Mother into the group and she introduced him around. Craddoc and Sam shook hands and I whispered to Jenny that I had to go to the john. While we combed our hair in the mirror, I asked Jenny how it was going.

"All right," she said. "Except Kenny would have loved tonight."

I agreed. When we got back to the auditorium, the crowd had thinned out and Craddoc told Mother if she didn't mind he'd like to steal me away for a while.

Out in the parking lot, Craddoc led me to his folks' station wagon. "Where's your little yellow VW?" I asked him after he let me in.

"Home. I thought this would be more comfortable for us tonight."

I looked around the inside. The back was put down flat. While he maneuvered us through the outgoing cars, I wondered how come he knew Tessie.

"Lots of guys . . . uh . . . people know Tessie."

"Did you know her when you were at school here and we were going together?"

"Did you know other guys besides me?" he countered. "How did *you* meet her?"

"I tutor her three times a week," I said, and then yelled, "Craddoc!" as he almost rammed the car stopping in front of us.

Craddoc didn't drive to our old spot overlooking the Sound. He drove to Woodway, wound around the tree-lined roads to his place, turned out the lights, and eased the car quietly down a side lane jutting into the foresty ten acres his family owns. He fiddled with the radio until he had soft music he wanted, then stretched back, giving me a wide smile. "You went to Planned Parenthood, huh?"

"No."

"No?"

"Craddoc, I didn't get up the nerve."

"What's nerve got to do with it?"

"It was too scary, that's all. I've never been in there."

"Elsie, you're seventeen years old."

"I know. I know. You keep telling me that." Our voices were getting loud.

Craddoc sat back against the seat. "Wait a minute. This isn't how it should go. Let's think about it. Now, you didn't go in because the place was strange?"

"Yes, I said in a whisper.

He took me by the shoulders. "Was there any other reason?"

"Not . . . not that I can think of."

He released me. "OK, then, we'll go tomorrow, together."

I swallowed. "I have to go to school tomorrow."

"We'll meet at your house right after school. I'll call and make the appointment."

"I tutor Tessie on Wednesdays."

"Not the last day before vacation, you don't." He looked at me closely through the dark of the car. "Elsie, you stand up and sing to a packed crowd without a quiver, but when we talk about us you turn to jelly. It's just me, Craddoc. Are you sure you love me?"

"I love you, Craddoc," I said, my voice sounding like a recording in my ears.

He gathered me close, and as we sat staring at the feathery outlines of the cedar trees, his words came dreamily into the night. "It seems like I've waited forever. I knew you were too young at fifteen. I thought maybe sixteen. Then my mother said you were a young sixteen."

"You talked this over with your mother?"

"No, she just happened to say that you were a smart, but a young, sixteen."

That didn't make me feel too great.

His arms tightened around me. "Anyway, I thought, When she's seventeen. That will be OK. That will be the time. What do you think?"

I wasn't about to admit I was a young seventeen. I mumbled that I didn't know.

His body sagged. "Don't you want me?"

"Any girl would want you, Craddoc." I reached up and stroked his face, trying to erase the hurt reflected in his voice.

Before I left school the next day, I stopped by the special ed classroom to be certain Tessie didn't expect me. She was waiting.

"Since this is the beginning of vacation, I didn't think we'd work this afternoon," I told her.

"I just came by to bring you this."

I took the small package from her and opened it. She had given me a gold-colored safety pin.

"It's to pin on your shawl on your

shoulder," she explained. "I wanted to thank you for helping me."

"I get a credit for doing it, you know."

"I know, but you teach me better than any teacher. You try harder."

"Well, thank you, Tessie." I wrapped the pin back up in the tissue paper and put it in my purse. "Can I drop you off somewhere? I've got my car out in the lot."

"No, I can still catch the bus. I hope you have a merry Christmas."

"You, too." I followed her out, thinking, If she'd only do something with that hair. . . .

Craddoc met me at my house, right on the dot. He was all hearty and cheerful and gabbed away to Robyn while I dumped my books. I was cheerful, too, on the drive to Planned Parenthood. I had had a midnight talk with myself and I was *not* going to be a baby about this.

The receptionist told me to fill out forms and wait my turn in the lobby, just like in any doctor's office. The whole thing took about three hours. First there was counseling, then the lab work, and then the physical examination.

Craddoc was slouched in a chair flipping through *House Beautiful* when I came back into the lobby. "Let's get out of here," I told him.

"Well," he said when we were out in his car, "you all set?"

"Yes."

"What would you like to do tonight?"

"Not much. I can't be 'sexually active' for a month."

"Why a month?"

"The pills have to have time to work."

He started up the car slowly. "Why didn't you get something —"

"I don't want to talk about it."

"Elsie, I can —"

"I don't want to talk about it, I said."

We rode silently to my house. He sat for a minute with his hands on the steering wheel. "What worries me is the way you're reacting to this."

"I've never acted the way you think I should, have I?"

"This isn't like your old paranoid fits. They made me feel bad, but I knew you wanted me. Now I'm not so sure."

His bewilderment was coming through to me, bringing an invasion of the old guilt. "I don't understand me, either," I said. "Can't we have a merry Christmas, anyway? Remember, you said you'd come to my house for Christmas Eve dinner."

"Right, and I'll call you later about tonight. Maybe we'll go to a show." He kissed me good-bye and I got out of the car and walked up to my door with my head bent to avoid the rain.

12. On the Hunt Again

Two days before Christmas, while Robyn and I were trying to get the tree to stand up straight in our living room, Jeanne called and asked me to baby-sit. I tried to talk her out of it because I had all my presents and I wanted to spend the afternoon putting decorations on the tree.

"Please come over just for a couple of hours," Jeanne pleaded. "I forgot Ed's secretary's present and he has to give it to her tomorrow."

"He's a grown man," I told her. "Let him buy his own presents. Call him up and tell him to get her a box of candy on his way home."

"No, he said for me to pick her out an evening purse. He heard her say she wished she had one."

"That's stupid. The stores are open till nine this week and he probably knows what color she'd want better than you do."

"He told me to get her a black one. It's just

for a few hours, Elsie. Teddy's sleeping and I'll be back by dinnertime."

I gave in. I don't know why. The whole thing was so dumb.

"If I had a car, I'd sure go for the money," Robyn said.

"You can start earning the money for a car next summer. Make Jeanne pick you up before work and take you home like I did. The job's yours."

Robyn followed me to the door as I was yanking on my jacket. "What'll you do next summer?"

"I'll find work somewhere."

The mailman had come and there was a letter from Jack. I stuffed it in my pocket and handed the rest of the junk to Robyn.

"Listen," Robyn called after me as I walked down the front steps. "Get some more red baubles. The tree looks pretty big."

The tree *was* pretty big. We wanted it that way. This was going to be the best Christmas Eve ever.

Jeanne hadn't lied. Teddy was sleeping. After she left, I cleaned the magazines, orange peels, and newspapers off the davenport and sat down to read Jack's letter.

Hello Elsie,

I just finished reading your letter. All of the turmoil inside of you really came through. I know what you mean about coming together. Especially since only a short time ago I felt I might make a wrong move at any moment and end up in trouble.

The last few weeks living at my parents' house were really a nightmare. The tension of not knowing what to do just about made me burst. One night I was lying in bed unable to sleep. I saw my life like a huge ladder stretching up as far as I could see and I hadn't even reached the bottom rung.

Elsie, I felt totally trapped. I was just too bummed out on school to go back. Looking for a job near home was hopeless, and besides, I don't even have a car. I thought I would be able to go work with my uncle in Alaska, but the fishing wasn't any good. When Kevin called and offered to let me come live with him and try to find a job, I was almost too petrified to come over here.

Last week, while I was eating breakfast at the Kalaloch Lodge, I was talking to Richard about getting stuck in indecision. Richard lives in one of a bunch of cabins called the Ghetto. (If you saw the place, you would know why everyone calls it the Ghetto.)

Gretta, a fourteen-year-old girl who lives across the street from Richard, has fallen madly in love with him. Richard, who is nineteen, claims he's in love with her, too. The problem is, Gretta has been sneaking over to his house and her father found out. Her father is a rough and tough logger. He told Richard if he caught him with her again, he'd beat him to pulp.

We were talking about Richard's problem and how to know the right thing to do, when this logger overheard us and handed out some friendly advice.

He said, "If you don't know what to do, just do something and you're bound to find out if it's wrong or right."

I was thinking advice like that could really mess somebody up as I watched Richard, who was completely bummed out, listening to this guy.

The sun is starting to set now, and I want to watch it, so I'll be back in a bit.

Watching the sun melt in the Pacific was totally shining. I wish you could have been with me to see it. Sometime you should come over here for a visit and see what I mean.

While I was looking at the sunset, I thought about what you said in your letter about feeling power. I feel more in control of my life now than ever before. I'm supporting myself, making my own decisions, and it feels great.

I guess I better go to bed now. I had a really rough day and I could use a good night's sleep. Maybe Lisa's baby won't keep me awake tonight.

I think of you all the time,
Jack

Hmmm. He thinks of me all the time, huh? Jack had never come right out and said anything like that to me before. I sat imagining Jack wearing the big black boots I'd bought him until Teddy came toddling out from his nap, soaking wet.

Jeanne didn't get home until seven in the evening, which figures. She dumped her packages down on the coffee table and asked me where Dad was. I didn't know. Without taking off her rain-soaked coat, she marched to the phone and called his office. No answer. "Where the hell is he?"

I raised my palms in innocence. I didn't know. I would have liked to ask her what his secretary looked like, but she was in no mood for that.

She put her hands on her hips and stared angrily at the front door. "He told me he'd be home on time tonight, so I thought I could shop a little longer and let him take care of Teddy and you could leave early."

Fat chance, I thought to myself.

Teddy came in from the kitchen, still chomping on a piece of apple I'd given him. "Mama!" He threw his arms around her legs and Jeanne gave him a sharp shove.

"Go wash your sticky hands."

Teddy studied his hands. "Not sticky." Then he spied the packages. "Pwesents." He pulled up the edge of a Nordstroms' sack and peeked inside.

"I told you to wash your hands!" Jeanne

knocked Teddy away from the coffee table. He landed with his head against the corner of the TV and started to howl. She grabbed him by the arm and yanked him to his feet. "When I tell you to do something, you do it! You hear me?"

Teddy cringed from her in terror as she shook him like a rag doll.

"Wait a minute. *Wait* a minute!" I got off the davenport, lifted Teddy away from Jeanne, and carried him into his bedroom. I sat on his little bed hugging him and rocking him back and forth until his sobbing quieted.

He looked up into my face with his sad, wet eyes. "E'sie, Mama hit Teddy."

"I know, love. I know." I leaned my cheek against his soft baby hair and tried to still my sickened stomach. Searching through my jeans pockets, I pulled out a package of Certs. "Here, here's a present for Teddy." While he was busy unwrapping the foil, I stalked into the living room.

"If you ever, ever," I told Jeanne through clenched teeth, "take your miseries with Dad out on Teddy again, I will never baby-sit for you and I will also see to it that you do some explaining to a child-abuse worker."

Jeanne kept herself preoccupied with getting a ten-dollar bill out of her purse. "You just are too young to understand how upset a woman can get when she's worried about her husband."

"Don't you believe it!" I snatched the money out of her hands and got out of there.

I don't know exactly how I got home, but it was lucky no cops were around. Halfway there, I remembered the ornaments Robyn wanted and did a left turn in the middle of the road and skidded up to the Pay 'n' Save. A middle-aged man yelled at me out of his car window and he got a finger in return.

I was cooled down a bit by the time I reached my house, but it was lucky for Mother she wasn't home. Robyn was carefully clipping glass birds onto the tree. I tossed her the package of red balls.

"Ummm." She eyed me closely. "What happened at Jeanne's?"

"She's finding out that Dad goes on the hunt, and she's taking it out on Teddy."

"Oh." Robyn pulled the box out of the bag I had given her. "There's some dinner in the oven, but I guess you don't feel much like eating, huh?"

"You're right."

"Craddoc called and said he had to visit relatives with his folks tonight but he'd be here tomorrow night for dinner."

"That's good." Both ways it was good. I was glad I didn't have to go out that night and I was glad Craddoc was remembering Christmas Eve. I took off my jacket and dragged it behind me as I headed for my room to lie on my bed and try not to remember the times when I had been in little Teddy's place.

13. It Was Christmas, After All

Robyn and I had planned baked ham, yams, string beans with toasted almonds, avocado and grapefruit salad, French rolls, and ice cream topped with warmed mincemeat for our Christmas Eve dinner. As soon as we finished breakfast, I boiled and sliced the yams into a buttered baking dish while Robyn peeled and sliced sections of grapefruit into a bowl. We stored our prepared food in the refrigerator, and after we cleaned the house, Robyn popped popcorn while I got out the cranberries and the big needles and thread. By three o'clock we were settled down together on the living-room floor, stringing the last of our decorations for the tree.

"I had a weird dream last night," Robyn told me. "I dreamed you and I were on a sandy beach and there were logs along the beach and Jack was there and all through the dream I kept worrying — not exactly worrying, but thinking that you might make a mistake."

I stood up to drape my first string of cranberries over the limbs of the tree. "What kind of mistake?"

"I don't know. It had something to do with Jack. I woke up thinking about it, and I thought I'd remember everything, but most of it evaporated."

"You're supposed to write your dreams down."

"I know." Robyn draped her popcorn on the tree and then we both took up the stringing again.

"I wonder," Robyn said after a while, "if Mother will marry Sam."

I thought about that.

"I wouldn't like someone to start bossing us around and having to put a robe on every time we went to the bathroom in the middle of the night."

Just what I was thinking. There was a knock on our front door and I got up to answer it.

"Merry Christmas, Elsie."

There he stood, a foot taller than me and with shoulders about three feet wide. "Jack! I can't believe it. You look so different! Come on in. Let me take your jacket. Ohh, Jack!" I dropped the jacket he'd handed me on the floor and threw my arms around him. Pulling back, I searched his face, trying to figure out why he looked older. "It's that mustache!"

Robyn had stopped stringing popcorn and was staring at him, too. "What are you doing? Pumping iron twice a day?"

"Forty cords of waterlogged cedar blocks are a bit heavier than a barbell set. *You* sure grew up quick. I bet you have trouble keeping the boys down."

Robyn grimaced. "Don't I wish."

I picked up his coat and threw it over a chair. "Come on, sit down." I patted a place beside me on the davenport, wondering about the little white box he was holding in his hand.

"Here, I brought you this."

"You did!" I loosened the pink ribbon and unwrapped the tissue paper. Robyn eased over to watch. Inside the box was a fragile silver bracelet with a turquoise stone set in the center. "Oh, Jack, it's gorgeous."

"Here, let me help you. You have to bend it to fit." Jack slipped the bracelet on my wrist and pressed it closed with his strong hands.

"I can't get over it. You're so changed." I didn't remember his hands being that large.

Robyn leaned down to get a better view. "It looks like it was made by Indians."

"Could be," Jack said. "I bought it at the craft shop in Forks."

"I got you a little something, too." I left for my bedroom and came back out with the huge package. "I hope they fit."

"How'd you know I was going to be in town?" he asked me as he tore away the wrappings.

I smiled at him. "I just knew."

He pulled out the big black boots and set them in front of him.

I could feel my face beaming. "Well, how do you like them?"

"They're great. I needed something to wear after work."

"After work?" I sat down next to him with a thump. "I got them so you'd be dry in the woods."

"I have to wear caulks in the woods, but don't worry. I'll get plenty of use out of these. The logging trucks churn up piles of mud in front of our house and my tennis shoes don't cut it."

"Try them on. See if they fit," I told him.

Jack stuffed his stocking feet into the boots and strode around the room. "They fit perfectly."

Robyn got the bowl of popcorn and settled on the floor in front of the davenport. "What are caulks?" she asked when Jack sat back down.

"Caulks are sturdy waterproof leather boots. The tops almost touch my knees and they have steel spikes on the bottom."

"What are the steel spikes for?" I asked.

"I run around on top of slimy wood all day. The steel spikes stick to the wood like Velcro." Jack reached down to take the rubber boots off. "Thanks a lot, Elsie. These sure beat muddy tennis shoes."

"What's the Shaman doing for Christmas?" Robyn wanted to know.

"Probably the same as everybody else," Jack said.

"How come?" Robyn screwed her face up like she does when she's perplexed. "He isn't a Christian, is he?"

"I doubt if Steve looks at it like that. I think he'd feel the birth of any spiritual teacher was important."

The grandfather clock bonged four times. "Oops. Excuse me a minute, Jack. I've got to get the ham in the oven."

"Would you like to stay for dinner?" I heard Robyn say as I went into the kitchen.

I dumped the ham in the roasting pan, smeared mustard and brown sugar over it, and poked it full of cloves, while trying to listen to the conversation in the living room. I heard Jack ask who was coming and Robyn say Sam was going to bring Mother home after the office party and pick up Grandma, and Cecile should be over pretty soon and Craddoc was coming.

Oh, oh. That would do it. I shoved the ham in the oven and hurried into the living room as Jack was getting up. "You don't have to go yet, do you? Can't you stay a while longer and visit? I haven't seen you for six months."

"No, I really have to get back home. I'll be around until New Year's Day, though."

Disappointed, I put my hand on his shoulder as he opened the front door. "Don't I at least get a good-bye hug?"

He held the boots in one arm, grabbed me

around the waist with the other, gave me a swift, hard hug, and was gone.

Robyn was crestfallen. "I shouldn't have mentioned Craddoc so soon, right?"

"Probably not. Come on, let's set the table."

The table was sparkling and the tree was sparkling by the time Cecile and Craddoc arrived. While Cecile and Robyn exchanged friendship rings, Craddoc looked over our decorations, grinning like a big Cheshire cat.

I poked him. "What's with you?"

He opened his eyes wide. "Ready for Santa Claus?"

"Sure."

He hopped out the front door and hopped back in, holding a package three feet long.

"What is it?" I said.

"Guess."

"I can't even begin to guess."

"A guitar!" Robyn shouted.

I looked at her as if she were crazy.

Craddoc handed me the present and I put it on the floor and tore off the patched-up wrappings. "Oh, no!" It *was* an instrument case. I opened the case slowly. Inside was a gleaming acoustical guitar. "Oh, no!" Tears flooded my eyes as I carefully lifted the guitar out of its case.

"You're not supposed to cry," Craddoc said.

"But it's so beautiful."

"Gawd, it is," Cecile said. Both she and Robyn were hovering over me.

Robyn reached down and stroked the sides. "What kind of wood is that?" she asked Craddoc.

"The neck's rosewood and the body's spruce. You have to have a hardwood like mahogany or rosewood for the neck."

"I bet it set you back some bucks," Cecile said.

I stared up at Craddoc apprehensively. "It does look terribly expensive."

"Well, I got a deal." He was obviously proud of himself. "One of my fraternity brothers had it, but he didn't have an ear and couldn't learn to tune it. I knew you could, so I waited around until he was short of cash for Christmas and then offered to buy it off him."

I picked at the strings. "It sounds in tune now."

"That's because I took it down to Kennelly-Keys this morning and had them tune it for me."

I reluctantly put the guitar on the coffee table. I hated to let it out of my hands. Robyn leaned forward. "Don't touch," I warned.

"I can see you're going to be a big pig," she said.

"You're so right." I retrieved my present for Craddoc from under the tree. "It's not nearly as grand as what you gave me."

He opened my gift of a tan suede wallet. "It's great," he told me, taking out his old wallet from his back pocket to exchange the contents. "I really needed a new one."

I was relieved to see he did. His old one was

worn at the seams and the plastic cardholder was cracked. I got out my folk-song book and practiced fingering chord positions until Mother, Sam, and Grandma arrived.

Everyone enjoyed our dinner — except Grandma, of course. Robyn passed her the platter of ham. "Have some, Grandma."

"No, I detest ham." She looked reproachfully at Mother. "It seems like you could remember my tastes for the two times a year I get invited to dinner."

Sam took the platter from Robyn, forked a small piece onto Grandma's plate and two big pieces onto his own plate, and passed the platter to Craddoc.

"I hate that red stuff," Grandma said, wrinkling her nose.

Sam put an arm around her. "Ah, come on now, Dorothy. It'll put hair on your chest."

"I don't want hair on my chest!"

We all laughed and Grandma couldn't hide a little smirk while she sat looking like an aged doll in Sam's embrace.

The rest of the dinner went fine — at least I thought it did — until I was serving dessert. Grandma focused on my turquoise bracelet as I set a plate of ice cream in front of her. "That's pretty. Is that what Craddoc gave you?"

"No, he gave me the guitar. This is from another friend." I moved over to serve Sam.

Grandma's beady eyes followed me. "So you have *two* boyfriends, do you?"

Without answering her, I hurried into the kitchen to pick up more plates of ice cream, which Robyn had topped with warm mincemeat. "Grandma's a real joy," I muttered before returning to the dining room.

"Really," Robyn agreed.

I glanced quickly at Craddoc's face before I began my dessert.

"Jack give you that gold chain you wear around your neck, too?" he asked me.

"Yes, for my birthday."

Sam took that moment to tell a funny story about a buyer who wanted to purchase a two-hundred-thousand-dollar duplex with no down payment. After dinner he suggested Mother and he do the dishes since we girls had gotten dinner.

"We may keep you around, Sam," Robyn told him.

I sat on the davenport chording "Down in the Valley" while Robyn and Cecile picked out the best pieces of candy from the box of chocolates Grandma had brought. Craddoc wandered into the kitchen to talk Rose Bowl with Sam. He and his parents were leaving for Pasadena after their Christmas Day celebration.

When the dishes were finished, Craddoc joined me on the davenport. I was wearing a white wool dress that was embroidered around the square neck and fell straight to my knees from the snug bodice. Craddoc stroked the wide sleeves. "You look like a

Christmas angel in that dress." The tender, vulnerable expression on his face made me put the guitar aside to kiss him.

Mother sat down at the piano. "How about 'I Heard the Bells on Christmas Day'?"

"Aw right!" Robyn and Cecile said together, and we all joined Mother at the piano to sing Christmas carols.

Craddoc and Cecile left about nine o'clock. At the door, Craddoc held me close and ran his fingers lightly over my hair. "I'll be flying home for my mother's birthday on Sunday, January twenty-ninth. If I stay over till Monday, will you skip school and take me to the airport in the afternoon?"

"Sure I will."

"And will you learn a love song and play it to me in the morning?"

"I'll play you a love song," I promised.

Our family gathered around the tree to exchange presents after Cecile and Craddoc had gone. Mother gave Robyn and me Frye leather boots, which we immediately pulled on. But the gifts Robyn and I liked best were from Sam. He gave each of us a crisp hundred-dollar bill. "Whoa!" Robyn shouted when she received hers. "This will be my first savings deposit toward a car."

"This will be my whole deposit on a set of snow tires," I said.

"It better be," Mother agreed. "You can't luck out all winter on the weather."

Grandma started to hate her presents, as usual, but when she opened Sam's card and discovered she had a hundred-dollar bill, too, her eyes lit up.

Then Mother opened my gift to her, the gray leather purse. "Oh, my. Oh, my, it's simply beautiful." She held it in the air, looking from me to Sam, and then back to me. "Oh, Elsie, this must have taken two months of your baby-sitting money."

It came to me that part of her joy was in Sam's seeing what a lovely present I had given her. She leaned over to give me a kiss of thanks and I let her. It was Christmas, after all.

14. A Lady Wouldn't Eat in a Place Like This

Around two o'clock on Christmas Day I took the record I had bought for Jenny and drove over to her condominium in Edmonds. I'd given her an album for her birthday, too, but that's what she likes best. Kenny met me at the door. "I didn't expect you," I told him. "When did you move in?"

"I didn't," he said. "Dad and I just came up for Christmas."

"Well, Merry Christmas!"

"Sure." He walked slowly into the living room, with me following him.

Jenny, her mom, Einer, Diane, and Rick were gathered around the large coffee table playing a new board game. I sat down on the davenport behind Jenny, and Kenny settled himself under the tree to take up the battle on his toy computer. Mr. Sawyer was sitting in a chair by himself at the other end of the room, gazing out the big windows at the ferries crossing Puget Sound. He looked sort of shriveled and out of it in the handsome new place.

Mrs. Sawyer passed me a bowl of Christmas candy and told me I looked beautiful in the shawl Jenny had given me for my birthday. Rick gave me a quick once-over with one eyebrow raised.

"Remember Marianne?" Diane asked me when her turn at the board had passed. "She was in school with us until she moved to Denver in the seventh grade?"

I remembered her. She was the first girl who befriended me in fifth grade and the one who was always special to Jack. "What about her?" I asked.

"We passed her on the way here. She honked at us and we pulled over to talk to her. She asked the directions to Jack's house. Her family's in town for the holidays and she wanted to see him."

"What does she look like now?"

"She's still petite," Diane told me. "And still pretty, with those big gray eyes and turned-up nose."

"Come on." Rick put his hand under Diane's bottom and lifted her up. "Jenny's mom's got us beat, so let's check in on my dad."

"We just left him an hour ago," Diane protested as Rick tossed her her coat.

"That's OK. I don't like to leave him alone too long." He nodded to everybody and steered Diane out by her hips while she was still trying to say her good-byes.

That little scene was a change from the bossy Diane I knew. And I bet there was no arguing about the pill, either.

The game broke up, and I gave Jenny her present and she took me into her bedroom to get mine. "Any hope for a reconciliation?" I asked her.

"Not a chance." She nodded toward the suitcases by the bed. "Dad and Kenny slept in here and I slept with Mom."

I perched on the edge of Jenny's rocker and unwrapped a jasmine plant that was covered with tiny white buds.

"Hang it in your window, away from a heater," Jenny said, "and it will make your whole bedroom smell delicious when it blooms."

I carefully carried the plant out to the living room by its hanger to say good-bye to everyone. Mrs. Sawyer hugged me; Einer was over talking to Mr. Sawyer, which I thought was nice of Einer; Kenny barely noticed when I touched his shoulder and wished him another Merry Christmas.

I drove home feeling glad and sad. Glad for the pretty jasmine plant and sad because happy, inquisitive Kenny was now a withdrawn little kid. I really like Jenny's mother, but there must have been some other way than giving up Kenny. Even *my* mother wouldn't have done that.

The rest of Christmas vacation wasn't much. Jenny was mostly occupied with Einer and her family, Mother with Sam, and Robin with Cecile. I read books (a fantastic novel called *The Color Purple*), took the tree down, and cleaned up the house. Being alone didn't really get to me until New Year's Eve.

Robin and Cecile were at a horror movie, Mother and Sam were at a dinner dance, and where was Jack? He could have at least called me. Even if he was with Marianne, she was no excuse not to say good-bye to me.

I sat in Mother's chair, slipped off my moccasins, and dug my toes into Honey Bear's deep fur. Where was Jack? I didn't let myself think it over when I caught myself dialing his number.

"Hello, Elsie," he said.

"How did you know it was me?"

"I just knew."

"You were leaving without saying good-bye."

"No, I wasn't. I planned to call you tomorrow before I left."

"So I don't even get to see you again before you leave. Some friend." I tried to keep from sounding pitiful.

"Well, I figured you would be busy with the holidays and all. Where are you? Where's Craddoc?"

"Craddoc's in Pasadena at the Rose Bowl and I'm home entertaining Honey Bear."

"So what do you want to do? Stay there and snivel?"

"Of course."

"I'll tell you what. I don't feel like partying, but I would like to see a play called *Bent*. I read a book a couple of weeks ago about the concentration camps during World War II. *Bent*'s about the persecution of gays in those concentration camps. It's playing at the Empty Space Theater on Capitol Hill. My folks are having a party here tonight, so if you want to go, I'll borrow their car and pick you up at seven o'clock."

"I'll be ready," I said.

The Empty Space Theater is on the second floor of an obscure building on Pike Street in Seattle. Jack drove around the block three times before we spotted it. He held my hand as we dashed up the narrow stairs to the ticket window and got two of the last seats in the house.

We were seated in the front row, about three yards from the stage, which was the floor in front of us. The whole theater was painted black, and a maze of lights and wires hung from the ceiling above. The theater darkened, there was a pause, and the lights focused on a scene in an apartment in Berlin. The two men living together were talking when a stranger, whom one of the men had brought home the night before, walked across the stage looking for the bathroom. The stranger wore no clothes.

After the first act, Jack looked over at me. "Well, how do you like it so far?"

"Weird! That's the first time I've ever seen a man bare-naked ten feet in front of me."

"You're kidding. Where've you been?"

"Living with my mother and sister. What did you think?"

In the last act of the play, the men were imprisoned by the Nazis and forced to carry piles of rocks back and forth, back and forth, in the hot sun. "What stunned me," Jack said later on our drive home, "was the way the sweat pouring off the actors made you really believe it was boiling hot out."

"What stunned me," I said, "was that the last man alive decided to run into the electric fence rather than give the Nazis the power to kill him."

"Those concentration camps were totally horrendous, you know. In *The Informed Heart*, the book I was telling you about, Bruno tells how he arrives at this concentration camp half-dead. He's so wasted he can barely eat. An old prisoner tells him he better eat whatever and whenever he can and to be constantly doing something if he wants to survive. So Bruno starts analyzing the other prisoners to keep himself occupied and finds out that the prisoners who stayed alive made decisions about what they did, even if they could only do it in their minds. The ones who became zombies and died were the ones who gave up doing anything to affect their lives.

"Bruno figured it wasn't important only to stay alive, but also to keep a sense of humanity. The secret to surviving as a human being in the concentration camps was to choose your own attitude and to inform your heart why you acted in a certain way. That's why he called his book *The Informed Heart*."

I mulled this over most of the way home. "Where'd you get the book?" I asked Jack as we neared my house.

"In the Forks library. The title caught my eye. I thought it was pretty interesting because some of it matches what I've heard Steve talking about lately."

I took Jack's hand when he walked me up my front steps. On my porch I could feel he was ready to say good-bye and I didn't want to let him go. Horns and guns blasted off into the night. "It's twelve o'clock. You have to give me a New Year's kiss."

I slipped my arms around his neck. His face turned solemn as he bent his head to kiss me. The kiss was stingingly sweet and my arms tightened as he drew me close against him.

The door behind us banged open. "Craddoc's on the phone to say Happy New Year to — Ohh. . . ." Robin's voice dribbled off.

Jack took me by my shoulders, turned me toward the door, and told me to answer the phone. After I said a hurried Happy New Year back to Craddoc, I rushed out to the porch, but Jack was gone. Knowing Jack, I knew I wouldn't be hearing from him again soon. And I didn't.

At school, my classes were continuously boring and I began to think my math teacher was right in suggesting I hurry up and get out of there. I made a little headway tutoring Tessie. Still, some days she got it and some days she forgot it. I figured by February I should have her in shape to pass the math competency test she needed to graduate — if it came on a day she was functioning.

About the middle of January, when Tessie was solving a decimal problem on the blackboard, I said to her, "You know, your hair might look real cute short and curled around your head."

"Do you think so?" She pulled on the oily strands with one hand. "I know it looks awful."

"Why don't I cut it for you and give you a permanent?" I said this without thinking.

"OK," she agreed. "I've got some money to get a home kit. Can we go to my house and do it now?"

So we went to her house. It was a dump. A filthy dump. Her mother was sitting in the living room on a broken-down couch swilling wine when we came in. "Why, hello, dear," she said after Tessie reintroduced us. "Tessie didn't warn me that she was bringing home company or I would have tried to straighten up this mess. I haven't been well at all lately."

"That's too bad," I murmured.

"Elsie's going to cut my hair short and give me a permanent," Tessie said.

"How nice for you. You'd better heat some water first."

Tessie glanced at the TV, which was babbling away to itself. "The electricity's on. Good. Come on, Elsie."

Heat water? Electricity's on? I followed Tessie into the kitchen, where she rinsed out one of the pans in the sink, filled it with water, and lifted it onto the grimy stove.

"The water heater broke last year and we don't have the money to fix it," Tessie explained.

How many bottles of wine would it take to cover the cost of a water heater?

I managed to get Tessie's hair clean by soaping it in the bathroom sink and pouring warm water on her head while she leaned over the bathtub. I cut her wet hair about two inches long all over her head and wound it up on small curlers. We sat on her bed while we waited for the permanent to take. I tried to ignore the gray sheet and the slipless gray pillow that was punched into a limp ball.

When her hair was finished we showed Tessie off to her mother. "My, you look like a TV star," her mother said, and Tessie did, too. The red circle of curls highlighted her green eyes with their long, curly lashes.

Tessie pranced around the room waving her glowing head. "Stay for dinner, Elsie. We've got a frozen pizza, haven't we?" she asked her mother.

"Oh, no," I said quickly. "Thanks a lot, but it's time for me to be getting home."

Mrs. Jones's face tightened into a knot. "Of

course you do. A little lady like you wouldn't be eating in a place like this."

Tessie froze. "Elsie probably does have to get home, Mom. We can ask her another time, can't we? And you can make your famous spaghetti for her. Won't that be fun?"

"She isn't coming back. Nobody would if they weren't stuck in this broken-down trap." Mrs. Jones's head sagged on her chest and her hand reached out for the bottle.

"Well ... um ... I better be off. I'll see you tomorrow, Tessie. You sure look cute." I nodded to Mrs. Jones, who gave me a baleful stare as I eased out the door.

15. The Jail and the Hospital

I saw Tessie in the hall next day, on my way to second period. She was standing with one hip jutted out and her hand on the other hip and she was giving Rick and his friend a secretive half-smile while Rick's friend was coming on to her. All three of them obviously enjoyed her new look. I got put down by a drunk for that?

It was grade time again and Mr. Olson had me sit at a table in the counselors' area all second period to check off the names of the staff as they turned in their grade sheets. When the senior counselor gave me hers, I couldn't resist glancing down at the list of students with semester F's. Rick was there. An F in Algebra 3. I could have tutored him in that, easy. And if Mrs. Aaberg knew I was tutoring him, she probably would have agreed to an incomplete instead of an F at the quarter. Too bad he'd never told me what he was flunking. Of course, I could have asked.

Spilt milk. I smiled sweetly at the next teacher handing me his grade sheets.

Rick ambled in about a half-hour later and leaned on the table. "Getting ready to put the grades on the computer?" he asked.

"I'm not allowed to put them on," I said primly. "Mrs. Tabbs does that."

"That so?" He ambled on out.

To be that interested he *had* to need the credit.

I tutored Tessie again on Wednesday afternoon. It was one of her better days. Her mother must have laid off the bottle the night before. Or that morning. Anyway, as we were leaving the special ed area, I dared to give the opinion that maybe she ought to be careful about Rick's friend, as I figured him to be out just for a good time. She gave me her deadpan stare. "So am I," she informed me and went on her way.

You deserved that, stupid, I told myself. You weren't helping. You were interfering. You don't have any right to tell Tessie which way to go around the tree.

Friday afternoon, I baby-sat Teddy. Jeanne said she'd be home by five-thirty and she was. So was Dad. She told him he had his choice of playing with Teddy or getting dinner, since she couldn't do both at the same time. While I was stuffing my pay in my wallet, I heard Dad mumble a bit about needing a shower.

"So do I," Jeanne snapped. "All three of us

can take a bath together and we can send out for Kentucky Fried Chicken."

Dad allowed as how his shower could wait until bedtime and he told Teddy to get some of his books so he could read to him awhile. I'd already read to Teddy for an hour, but Teddy can listen to *Goodnight, Moon* forever and he happily wiggled up on his dad's lap with his books clutched to his chest.

I said good-bye to the little family and went out the door smiling to myself. Even though he parts his hair at the top of his ear and swirls it over his head, the fact is my once-handsome Dad is almost bald and Jeanne is twenty-nine. I think some leash yanking had taken place.

Saturday, I went over to Jenny's without calling first. It was Robyn's turn to clean the house and because it was the end of the semester I didn't have any homework. I felt restless and just got in my car and drove over. Jenny answered the door. "Have you heard?" she asked me.

"Heard what?" By the look on her face, the first thing I thought was that something had happened to Kenny or Einer.

"About Rick." She jerked her head toward the living room, where Diane was sitting on the davenport trying to stop up her tears with a wet ball of Kleenex.

I sat down on the nearest chair. "What's happened?"

"Rick's in jail." Diane's tears poured out again and Jenny went for a roll of toilet paper, unwound a long wad, and gave it to her.

I'd never seen Diane cry before. Never. Her face was swollen and blotchy and her eyes red and shrunken into wet slits. I knew her mother had had to scheme to acquire everything they needed since Diane's dad died, but to me Diane had always seemed to get where and what she wanted. Easily.

"Well, what happened?" I repeated.

Jenny settled on the davenport with Diane. "Rick and Darrel Norrison got picked up by the Edmonds police last night after they'd broken into the school. They got caught in the computer room while Darrel was working over the main computer."

Guilt oozed through my body as I watched Diane's mouth tremble. "It'll about kill Rick's dad," she said. "He's been getting sicker lately, anyway. And it's the end, the total end of Rick's chance for a scholarship and any chance for college."

"How long are they going to be locked up?" I asked.

Jenny's mom and Diane's mom came in the front door about then. Diane got up to meet them. She stood in front of her mother with her thumbnail pressed between her lower teeth and tears seeping down her cheeks. Her mother put an arm around her. "We got them both out on a personal recognizance. Rick's fine and we left him off at his house so he could be with his dad. Darrel's folks took him home."

Diane kept searching her mother's face. "What else?"

"Well." It was plain her mother was reluctant to go on. She brushed Diane's hair away from her damp forehead. "Oh, the two vice principals were at the station. I talked to Mr. Piker and Mr. Olson both. The boys will probably be suspended from school."

Diane sagged back onto the davenport.

"Now, girls," Mrs. Sawyer said. "This is an awful thing to have happen and it was incredibly stupid of Rick and Darrel, but it isn't the end of the world. More than one man has fallen on his face and picked himself up to make good on a new career. I'm going to make tea and sandwiches and maybe we'll all feel better."

Diane didn't look to me like any tea would make her feel better.

Monday, the whole school was buzzing with the news. I dreaded second period, and when I got to the computer room, Mr. Olson hustled me right into his office. "I assume you've heard that there was a break-in over the weekend?" he started out.

I nodded.

"The boys had the passwords to the computer."

I waited, my heart was thudding.

"One of the secretaries said she saw Rick Evers talking to you when you were collecting the grade sheets last week."

"He stopped by for a second," I said. "I know the girl he goes with."

"Hmmm." Vice principals have a way of swinging back and forth in their chairs that always make me shrink three sizes.

He waited too long this time, though. I felt guilty enough for having suggested putting the electric eye outside the computer room and I wasn't about to take on guilt for passing passwords that I didn't pass out. I stood up. "If you don't feel you can trust me, Mr. Olson, I think the best thing for me to do is drop my TA for spring semester and for you to reprogram the computer."

I was walking out when he restrained me with a hand on my shoulder. "Now, now, Elsie. No one's accusing you of anything. The boys told the police they got the passwords by watching the counselors' fingers as they typed them in. It seems to me that would be rather a difficult thing to do, but I've warned the counselors not to let the students stand behind them when they use their computers. Anyway, thanks to you, our surveillance led to their being caught and I think it's been a good lesson for all the students in the school, don't you?"

Oh, God, I got out of there.

Craddoc called in the evening, which didn't help my depression one bit. He wanted to remind me about his visit the next weekend. He said he'd fly in Sunday for his mother's birthday, have his dad drop him off at my house on his way to work Monday morning, and then we'd have the day alone together before I drove him to the airport for his three o'clock flight back. "Remember, it's been a month since Christmas," he added.

"I remember," I said.

Part of the week, I tried to forget Monday morning, and part of the week, I tried to find the book Jack had told me about, *The Informed Heart*. It wasn't in the card catalog at school, and when I inquired about it, the dumb librarian asked me if it was a romance novel.

Sunday night, I told Mother I was staying home from school the next day to be with Craddoc and take him to the airport. She didn't object, but I could see she was thinking it over. "I hope you know what you're doing," she said. I didn't tell her I didn't.

I had a hard time going to sleep. I woke up when my alarm usually goes off for school, lay there awhile, and then unexpectedly fell back to sleep. I awoke again with dread covering my body. I didn't move a muscle as the knowing crystallized in my head. Jack was hurt. Jack was hurt bad.

I threw off my covers and went for the phone in the living room. The operator said there was no Kevin Hanson listed for Clearwater. I put the receiver down. Maybe the phone was in Lisa's last name. I didn't know Lisa's last name. I was hurrying into my room to get Jack's letters to see if he had ever written down Grover's last name when there was a knock on the door and Craddoc stood there with a big grin on his face, holding a dozen roses.

"Come on in," I told him. "Jack's hurt."

"He is? How do you know?"

"I just know." I left him standing in the middle of the room while I scurried out to wash my teeth, pee, and grab up Jack's letters and a robe.

I sat on the footstool beside Craddoc's chair while I scanned each letter, then dropped it in a pile on the floor beside me. "Crap," I said. "He never wrote down Grover's last name." I called the operator again and asked her to give the number of the shake mill in Clearwater. When a man answered at the mill, the most I could hear was the screeching of saws in the background.

"Just a minute," he shouted, and a door slammed and the screeching faded. "Now what did you want?"

"I'm trying to find Jack Hanson. Do you know how I could reach him?"

"He doesn't work here anymore. He's working in the woods. He's probably out on a show now. I don't know if he has a phone. Sorry, lady."

"Thanks anyway." I hung up. "Now what am I going to do?"

"What am I going to do with these?" Craddoc said, holding the roses out to me.

"Oh, Craddoc, they're beautiful. I'll take them." While I was in the kitchen running water into a vase, I decided the only thing to do was to call Jack's mother. I'd feel like a fool, but it was the only thing left.

I set the flowers on the piano and dialed

Jack's number. I felt like a fool, all right. My persistence and desperation must have gotten to her, though, because she finally said she'd call the hospital in Forks and then call me right back.

I took my comb out of my purse and paced around the living room untangling my hair until the phone rang. Mrs. Hanson sounded a lot different than she had ten minutes before. "The hospital's been notified by radio that they're bringing in two injured men from the woods. We'll have to wait until they get to the hospital to find out their names."

"Is it all right if I come over?" I asked her.

"Please do," she said.

Craddoc was real quiet on the way over to Jack's house. He knew the Hansons, of course, because his family and Jack's family were longtime friends. Mrs. Hanson gave us cups of coffee and we waited and waited. About eleven o'clock, the hospital called back and said Jack was there, but they wouldn't know the extent of his injuries until the X rays were complete.

I started to cry. Mr. Hanson had arrived home by then, and he was the one who patted my back. He called the hospital again about twelve-thirty and was told Jack's lower back was injured, but they expected a full recovery.

I relaxed with relief and for the first time that morning focused on Craddoc. "Spoiled your happy day, huh?"

"That's OK," Craddoc said, "But we better be heading out."

We left Mr. and Mrs. Hanson packing up for a trip to Forks. Mrs. Hanson promised she'd call me as soon as they returned.

Craddoc was still pretty quiet on the long ride to the Seattle-Tacoma airport. I was keeping my eye on the snow flurries that were sticking to the windshield. I still didn't have my snow tires. When we passed Renton, he said, "Now explain to me how you knew Jack was hurt."

"I can't explain it. I woke up this morning with the awful feeling he was hurt, that's all."

When Craddoc was ready to board his plane, I kissed him good-bye, then grabbed him back for another hug, which I suppose in no way made up for his lost day.

The snow was really coming down on my trip home. I turned off the freeway at 175th and stopped at the OK tire store. It was dark before the overworked salesman got to my car in line. I told him I wanted two radial snow tires and he yelled for the tire buster to pull off my hubcaps. The tire buster was Rick. He didn't say anything to me and I didn't say anything to him as I stood shivering above him while he worked on his knees in the cold.

16. Inform Your Heart

The senior makeup test for math competency took place the next morning. Tessie came out of the testing session with her eyes dancing. She'd known how to do every problem and was sure she'd passed.

"That's great," I said. "Congratulations."

"To *you*." She brushed my arm gently. "I couldn't have done it without you." Her thanks left a glow over me for the rest of the schoolday.

Mrs. Hanson called in the late afternoon to tell me Jack was going to be fine. He would have to be in the hospital a few more days, then take it easy for a couple of weeks.

Was he coming home to recuperate? I wanted to know.

No, she said, he'd stay with Kevin and go back to work as soon as his back felt strong enough. But he sent his love to you, she added.

I hung up in tears. I don't know why. I wandered around the house feeling restless.

Outside, it was still snowing. It does that sometimes here late in the winter. Just when you think you can get away without putting snow tires on, it starts to come down. Despite the snow, I felt like doing something, so I left a note for Robyn telling her I wouldn't be home for dinner and I drove down to the public library in Seattle.

I had no trouble at all finding *The Informed Heart* there. Jack had referred to the author as Bruno. His full name is Dr. Bruno Bettelheim and there were five books by him, all sounding good. *Love Is Not Enough* and *The Informed Heart* were on the library shelf. I looked briefly at *Love Is Not Enough.* It was about the treatment of emotionally disturbed children. I think I would like to work with those children someday. I took *The Informed Heart* to a desk to read, since I didn't have a Seattle library card.

It is a fat book and I didn't finish it in the three hours I was there. My situation was nothing compared to the Holocaust, but before my eyes were too tired to read anymore, I did understand that Bettelheim believed you had a personal responsibility for your own acts and that you needed to choose your own attitude toward an action and inform your heart. That left me a bit lacking. I not only hadn't chosen an attitude about going to bed with Craddoc, I had avoided thinking about it. I closed the book with a *thwack*.

By the time I turned off the freeway toward

Lynnwood, the snow was coming down so fast I had to lean forward to see clearly out my windshield. The car ahead of me slithered, and I pumped my brakes for a gradual stop. While I idled my car, waiting for the driver ahead to straighten out, I noticed something familiar about a person weaving down the sidewalk. I stared through the snow at him as he drew parallel to my car. It was Rick Evers. Staggering drunk.

The driver ahead managed to slip and slide up the block, and I shifted into gear. Wa-ait a minute, Elsie, you can't leave Rick behind in this weather. I slowed to another stop until Rick advanced alongside again; then I leaned over and opened the passenger door. "Want a ride?"

He wobbled up to the door and peered inside. "We-ell, Snow White."

"Can I give you a lift?"

He hesitated, the lids of his eyes hanging halfway down, before climbing in. I wasn't his favorite driver, I could see.

"Where you headed?" I asked him.

"Home. To Mountlake Terrace. That out of your way?"

"Nope, I live in Brier."

"Oh. I'da thought you'd live in Woodway. No, it's your boyfriend that lives there, isn't it?"

The smell of alcohol was filling the inside of my small car, but it was too cold to open the windows. I turned up the fan.

"I can walk, Snow White, if I'm contaminating your atmosphere." He lurched over to open his door.

I yanked on him with my right hand. "No! Not when I'm driving, you idiot."

"Then, why don't you stop the car?"

Trying to see through my snowy windshield and handle him, too, was making me nervous. "Just keep it together, Rick, and I'll get you home. What street do you live on?"

"I live on a little street in a little house. Only I can't live there much longer because I can't afford to live there alone."

I concentrated on getting through the center of Lynnwood, working around all the stupid drivers with slick tires. When I was free to realize that Rick was silent beside me, I looked over at him. His eyes were closed and his face sagged with grief. "What did you do today?" I asked.

"I took my dad to the hospital. I broke his heart and then I took him to the hospital. But you wouldn't know about being a crippled man's dream, would you? Sitting in his wheelchair watching me race with the ball on TV — that was his big thing. That was the only thing he had left. But you wouldn't know about disappointing people, would you, Snow White? You'd never get kicked out of school."

"I got kicked out in the fourth grade."

"You're shittin' me."

"Nope, I'm not. I stole out of the school kitchen and I stole kids' lunch money to buy candy."

He peered at me, as if through a fog.

"I was a compulsive eater," I explained.

"Why's that?"

"I guess because I *wasn't* anybody's dream. I almost got kicked out of fifth grade, too."

Rick shook his head slowly. "Sure doesn't show now. You must have really gotten it together."

"Ha! But you can."

He leaned back in his seat. "Ha, no way. I've screwed it up good. No scholarship for me." Then, "Pull up behind that yellow truck," he told me.

I pulled up, turned off the key, and faced him. "Why were you taking Algebra Three, anyway? You don't have to have it."

"You do to go to the U of W. And I was trying to impress the other colleges. I impressed them, all right."

"I could have tutored you in algebra, easy."

He looked into my eyes. "Can you imagine being the dumbest in the class and asking a smart blonde who thinks she's special for help?"

"I don't think I'm special."

"No, you're all right, Elsie." Rick put his hand on my shoulder. "Thanks for the ride."

I sat in the car watching him wobble across the lawn toward the dark shape of the little rented house he wasn't going to be able to keep. You're all right, Elsie? You're a liar, Elsie. I had, too, thought I was special. So special I put Rick down in my head without even bothering to find out his problem in class before trapping him.

I gave out a bitter laugh as I started up my car.

There was a letter from Jack waiting for me when I got home Wednesday. I didn't even take my jacket off before I sat down to read it.

Hello Elsie,

When my mom came to visit me, she told me how you phoned her Monday morning and told her I was hurt. She said you bugged her so much that she called the Forks hospital and found out I was being brought in. She couldn't understand how you knew. Nothing like interconnections, huh?

You're probably wondering how I'm doing. The doctor told me I have antrospondylolisthesis at L3 and L4. That means I messed up my lower back. I'm going to have to take it easy for a while. I got hurt during a flyout. I'll tell you what a flyout is so you'll know what I'm talking about.

After we get done cutting the cedar into two-feet sections, it's split into shake blocks. About 1,000 pounds of blocks are put in a stack with a rope wrapped around it. The stack is called a sling.

When there are enough slings, a helicopter is hired to fly the wood out. A thirty-foot cable hangs from the belly of the bird (that's what we call a heli-

copter). On the end of the cable is a hook the pilot can electrically control. He flies the hook to us, we slip the rope onto the hook, he lifts the sling up and carries it to the landing. He goes back and forth like that until all the cedar is out of the woods.

The day I got hurt, I was hooking slings out of a box canyon in the bottom of a valley. It was about 400 feet from where I was to the landing, most of it straight up. Phillip, the pilot, was really cookin on. He was ripping slings from the side of the valley above me and dumping them up on the landing.

I was pushing a sling together, with my back to the bird, when I heard a thwap and got knocked to the ground. It sounded like somebody stuck a pencil into a fan and felt like somebody jammed one in my back. I rolled over and looked up to see the bird coming down on top of me. The cable was swinging wildly, wrapped around the tail, and the tail rotor was gone.

I saw Phillip look down, see he was about to crash on top of me, and try to pull up. Without the tail rotor, he was sunk. When he applied force to the main rotor, the body of the helicopter spun in the opposite direction. As he rose up about 50 feet, he began to spin faster and faster. The bird started wobbling like crazy. Then it skimmed over a little ridge and crashed on the lip of the canyon. Phillip was trying to get out as the bird teetered on the edge. Before he could, it rolled off and out of my view. I heard it tumble down the side of the canyon, then slam into the bottom.

Suddenly it was totally quiet except for the sound of the turbine engine winding down. It reminded me of a siren. I got up in a state of shock, even though my back was killing me, and ran down the canyon. When I came to the scene, I was horrified at what I saw. Pieces were everywhere! The red light on the bird was still flashing and fuel was spilling onto bone-dry cedar slash. The turbine had broken loose and was lying on the ground. I was scared shitless the fuel was going to reach the hot turbine and explode.

I ran up to the cockpit, but Phillip wasn't in it. I looked frantically around and found him a little ways away in the bushes. There was blood coming out of his mouth.

I could hear Grover yelling at me from up above. He was shouting at me to turn the power off in the helicopter because a spark could set the fuel off. I rushed to the cockpit, but there were so many switches I was afraid I would flip the wrong one and cause an explosion. I ran back to Phillip and told him he was going to have to turn the power off. I helped

147

him to the cockpit, he reached out, flipped a switch, and the red flashing light went out.

Then Grover arrived and we carried Phillip up the canyon to a level spot. As soon as we set him down, my back gave out completely and I was forced to lie down, too. Check this out, Elsie, we were stuck in the bottom of that canyon for two hours before the park rangers came from Kalaloch with stretchers to carry us out.

It turned out the blood in Phillip's mouth was just his teeth, but his back was hurt so bad, they had to fly him to Seattle. What got me was a chunk of the tail rotor hitting my lower back. Now here I am, lying in the Forks hospital with my back driving me crazy and sharp pains shooting down my legs.

The nurse just came in, so I've got to stop now. She told me she would mail this letter for me. I'll say one thing for this place, they sure dish out the royal treatment.

Thanks for caring about me,
Jack

P.S. Guess who's busted up in the room next door? Poor Richard. He got Gretta pregnant.

17. That Same Sweet Sting

Tessie did pass the test, and I got a new student to tutor, a boy named Harry Thrasher, who had some kind of heart defect that kept him out of school a lot. He tired easily, but he had a sly humor and learned quickly, so the sessions were fun for me. That was about all that was fun in school.

I kept the TA with Olson because I knew I wanted to graduate early. I was polite — barely — and did the work mechanically. Even my usual zest for math and the coming spring concert shriveled. I was so restless I had to pin myself down to study to prevent knocking myself off the honor roll.

On a Friday night in the middle of February, Mother announced that she and Sam were going to Reno for the weekend. She wondered if we girls would be all right alone.

"I wish we had somewhere to go," Robyn said.

"Let's go to Clearwater and see Jack. He should be almost well by now."

"Aw right!" Robyn said.

"But where will you stay?" This was making Mother a little nervous. "Shouldn't you call first?"

"Jack's brother has a house. Mrs. Hanson said they don't have a phone, but I'll call her and get directions. We'll take sleeping bags and sack out on the floor. Right, Robyn?"

"Right," Robyn said.

Mother left about ten o'clock Saturday morning, and Robyn and I weren't far behind her. After we passed Aberdeen, Robyn kept the state map on her lap. The roads into Clearwater were rough and muddy. The houses drooped soggily and the yards were spongy. "Look," Robyn said, "those cabins have outhouses behind them."

"This must be the Ghetto Jack wrote about." I slowed to check the mailboxes because there weren't any street signs. "We're almost there."

"I hope they've got a bathroom. I gotta go."

They did. Lisa let us in. Jack was in Queets with Kevin, Lisa told us, and should be back any minute. She served us mint tea with honey while we waited.

Jack's face burst into a big smile when he saw us, and he hugged me tight. I was careful not to squeeze his back too hard. We all went to the Kalaloch Lodge for dinner. Gwenivere had the table spattered with cracker crumbs before we were served. Robyn and I had salmon and the rest ate chicken.

"You can get sick of salmon living out here," Lisa explained.

The dining-room windows looked out over a lagoon and the Kalaloch creek flowing into the ocean. "I could spend a bit of time here, easy," I said.

"You *can* spend time here, easy," Kevin advised me. "The lodge hires people for the summer months to clean their cabins along the ocean and to wait tables. Get your application in early. A place to live comes with the job."

"If there's anything we know how to do, it's clean," Robyn said. "How old do you have to be?"

"At least sixteen," Jack told her.

Back at the house, we played cards until bedtime. When I was down in my sleeping bag with the darkness around, the old restlessness came back. I could feel Jack was still awake. I wanted to reach out and touch him so bad it hurt.

The rustling of his shifting on the couch did it. I slipped carefully, silently out of my sleeping bag and crept across the dark room until I felt his blankets against my leg. My hand found the warmth of his bare shoulder and I kneeled down, putting my cheek against his cheek. Neither of us said a word.

Lisa's baby whimpered, coughed out a cry that swelled into a howl.

"What's the matter with that thing?" Robyn mumbled.

"She's probably wet," Jack said.

"Well, do something to her. She's keeping me awake." Robyn flopped against the floor.

I rose up, disgusted. "Where are the diapers?"

"Lisa's got them stacked on the little stool."

I fumbled for the chain on the lamp and found the diapers. I was bending over Gwenivere when Lisa opened the bedroom door.

"What are you doing to my baby?" she asked sharply.

"Changing her. She's soaked," I said through the safety pins in my mouth.

"Oh." Lisa walked over to stand above me.

"Lisa always thinks you're doing something to her baby," Jack said.

"No, I don't." Lisa sounded defensive. "It's just . . . I get confused when I first wake up."

"I'll say you do," Jack said.

I handed Lisa a dry Gwenivere and crawled into my sleeping bag. Rotten baby!

In the morning, Robyn and I packed our things behind the seat in my car before Jack took us to breakfast at the lodge. He ordered pancakes and bacon and eggs and juice. "Big-time spender," Robyn said.

"Insurance," Jack said, handing the waitress back the menus.

We were eating in the coffee shop that overlooked the dining room and the big windows. I watched a man come up the steps. He was wearing jeans, a wool shirt, and hiking boots like the other locals in the place, but there was something about his serene expression that caught my attention.

Jack stood up when he saw him, shook his hand, and introduced us. "Elsie, Robyn, this is Steve Four-Suns."

I wanted to poke Robyn to make her stop staring. I think she memorizes Jack's letters. Jack pulled out a chair and invited Steve to join us.

Before Steve got his first sip of coffee, Robyn asked him, "Do Shamans get to know things other people don't?"

"Hmmm." He looked at her thoughtfully. "I think they practice being open to knowing more than most people do."

"And just how do you do that?"

"Pay attention to dreams, for one thing."

Robyn crumpled her bacon on top of her eggs. "And what if you wanted to know something in particular about a person or a problem and you didn't get a dream about it? Then what would you do?"

Steve nodded politely to the waitress when she set his plate in front of him. He answered Robyn as he poured syrup over his pancakes. "I would probably walk in the woods until I found a tree that I felt good sitting next to, relax against it, and listen for a ringing or the sound of the wind or the ocean in my head."

"But what if you don't hear that?" Robyn persisted. "What if you think about being hungry or that the ground's cold?"

"Just let those thoughts pass on through. Bring back the person or the problem and wait quietly for a picture or words or a feeling that will help you." Steve took a bite of his pancakes. I was afraid his breakfast was going to get cold. "An easy way to know you're ready to receive is when you can't feel your hands anymore."

"I'll try that," Robyn told him. I thought I'd try it, too.

After breakfast, Jack, Robyn, and I wound down the wooden stairs to the beach, watching the waves tumbling on the sand in front of us. "Gr-eat!" I said.

"Really," Robyn echoed.

I held my hair back from my face, looking far out over the Pacific Ocean. "What a place to live."

Jack moved up beside me, the bulk of his down coat shielding me from the wind. "You could if you wanted to."

We walked along the beach. Robyn bounced beside us, jumping from log to log, until she stumbled on two women. The plump one had a camera slung around her neck, and the skinny one, bundled up in two thick home-made sweaters, had a large sisal bag at her feet.

Jack slowed our pace as we approached them. "How ya doin? Having fun?"

"Oh, yes," the skinny one answered, nodding. "We're having a wonderful time."

"Where're you from?" Robyn asked.

"We're from Holland. Is this all the bigger

the waves get? The travel brochures have pictures of gigantic waves."

"Sounds like typical advertising. Today's about normal, but during storms it can get pretty interesting," Jack said. "Well, we're going to wander on down the beach. Take care."

As we walked along, I danced away and back to Jack. "Seems like everybody would be happy here."

"There's rip-off types here just like anywhere. You want to hear what happened to me last Sunday?"

"Sure we do." Robyn moved in close for what was obviously going to be one of Jack's adventures.

"I was in the lodge eating lunch at the counter," Jack started out. "An old man was sitting about four places down. He kept staring at me. Finally, he came over to me and said, 'You're probably wondering why I've been watching you.'

"I told him I had.

"He said the reason he was staring at me was because I looked exactly like his son, who died a week ago. Then he asked me if he could sit beside me while he finished his lunch. I said sure. He went over and brought his plate and cup and set them on the counter next to me.

"While we ate he explained how he was having a very hard time coping with the death of his only child and asked me if it would be OK if he called me 'son.' He looked harmless enough, so I said sure. We talked for a while and he called me 'son' a few times and then got up to leave. Walking out the door, he said, 'See you later, son.'

"After a bit the waitress came over and handed me a check. I looked at the bill and it wasn't mine. I told her it was for that old guy.

" 'Well, your father said you were going to pay for it.'

"I told her he wasn't my father and she said, 'When he walked out the door he called you "son." '

"Then it dawned on me what this guy had done."

Robyn tugged on Jack's free arm. "What'd you do?"

"I wasn't going to let that guy rip me off. I jumped up and ran out of the lodge just as he was waiting to pull out onto the highway. I raced across the parking lot, hollering at him. He took off, so I ran alongside his car.

"The window was rolled down. I reached in and jerked the steering wheel to the side, forcing him off the road. He was trying to roll the window up, but before he could, I got the door unlocked and open. He kept pushing me away as I tried to yank him out of the car. Then he started kicking me with his feet. I grabbed ahold of his leg and started pulling real hard — just like I'm pulling yours."

Robyn tackled Jack first. We managed to get him down on the sand, but he was too strong for us to drag into the water.

"Jack, you haven't changed a bit!" I told him while we were climbing the stairs to the car. Then I remembered his injury. "Oh, we shouldn't have wrestled with you."

"Don't worry about it. I'm almost well."

On the way back to Lisa and Kevin's house, though, I made him drive so he wouldn't have Robyn bouncing around on top of him. We stopped at Queets General Store to fill up the gas tank and get some Dr Peppers. When we pulled up in front of the house, I got out with Jack. Before he could thank me for the visit, I slipped my arms around his neck. "Give me a kiss good-bye."

"Elsie."

"I don't care. Give me a kiss good-bye."

He shook his head slowly. "No, it's too much of a game for you and too much the real thing for me."

"It isn't a game with me, Jack."

"Then you have some decisions —"

"I know." I reached up and bent his head down. He kissed me reluctantly at first. Then he swung me tightly to him with one hand and held my chin with the other. I had wondered if the same sweet sting would seep through my body, and it did.

He let me go slowly and opened the car door. As I turned to get in, I saw Robyn on the other side, watching us, bug-eyed.

18. Letter Number Two

Mother and Sam were in the living room sitting on the davenport together when Robin and I arrived home from Clearwater. Mother's blue eyes shone like sapphires as she held out her left hand to us. There was a wide gold band on her third finger.

"Just what I need," Robyn said, "a stepfather!" Sam's eyebrows shot up and Robyn hurriedly touched his shoulder. "Only kidding."

As I welcomed Sam, I felt Mother watching my face, so I bent down and kissed her cheek. "He's a great guy and you deserve him."

She held my head close to hers with quivering hands. "Thank you, honey."

Before I climbed into bed that night, I spotted a letter on my desk. It was from Craddoc. I didn't really want to hear from him then and tore open the envelope reluctantly.

Dear Elsie,

I've been thinking about my last visit up there. The Prof in my Psych 102 class always asks if there are any questions before he begins his nine o'clock lecture. Today I raised my hand to ask if he thought it was possible for one person to know if another person had an accident 200 miles away when there hadn't been any contact between them for a month.

The Prof said there were numerous twin studies in which one twin appeared to know, consciously or unconsciously, what was happening to the other twin. For instance, one twin would be aware when the other twin was giving birth to a baby or would experience pain similar to labor contractions. He also said there was some evidence to indicate that people with close emotional bonds sometimes appeared to be aware if a catastrophic event happened to one or the other.

I know you and Jack have been friends for a long time. It seems strange, tho, that he was the one who interrupted the only time we had. But since you're so nervous about the whole thing, maybe one morning together wasn't such a good idea. So how about spending your Easter vacation over here with me? One of my fraternity brothers has an apartment off campus and he's agreed (after much

*bribing, which included football-kicking
lessons six Saturday mornings) to stay
in my room at the house while we get his
apartment when you are here. Sound
good?*

*You're my girl, Elsie, and I don't want
to start up your paranoid imagination,
but I think we need to spend more time
together.*

*Write or call me to let me know when
you'll arrive so I can get everything
squared away. How would you like to
attend the psych class with me?*

Love,
Craddoc

I didn't need to be paranoid to imagine
college girls coming on to Craddoc. But the
point was, what did I want? Craddoc had
helped me trust. For two and a half years I'd
depended on Craddoc, basked in his reflected
light. Could I give that up? I tossed around
my bed half the night until I promised myself
I'd try the Shaman's problem-solving method
the very next day.

I dropped Jenny off at her house after
school and drove over to Woodway Park. I
left my car at the top of the hill and wandered
down through the woods until I found a big
fir tree that felt just right, sturdy with thick
green branches. I sat down at the bottom of
it and leaned against its trunk, trying to
relax. After about five minutes I peeked

through my lashes to see if anyone was watching.

No one was around. I settled closer to the tree and tried to hear wind in my head. No wind. I wondered if I looked weird sitting there, and peeked out again. I was alone. Come on, Elsie, get down to it. Picture Craddoc. Craddoc. Right?

I saw Craddoc on the phone trying to reason with me after I'd walked out on him at a party because I was having a jealous fit over his attentions to another girl. I saw Craddoc convincing me that it was fine for him to leave me sitting alone at a party, feeling lost and rejected. I saw Craddoc's jaw twitch when he didn't get his own way. I saw Craddoc's shining face as he gave me Honey Bear for my fifteenth birthday. I saw him explaining to Mother that Honey Bear was housebroken so Mother would let me keep my puppy. I heard Craddoc saying, "I trust you. Can you trust me?" I saw him kick the ball through the goalposts. I heard him telling me I should try harder to be social, try harder to be what he thought I should be.

I opened my eyes slowly. I cared for Craddoc but I didn't need him anymore. I wouldn't grow with Craddoc. I'd just be Craddoc's girl. An appendage.

Craddoc was my first love, my hero. Craddoc had tried to tell me he was Craddoc, just Craddoc. But his choosing me made me believe I was worth something.

And the sad thing for Craddoc was that

now that he had helped me grow strong, I wanted to be Elsie and decide about when and who I'd make love to.

And how do you write a "Dear John" letter, Mr. Shaman and Dr. Bettelheim, after you've informed your heart?

The letter took me a long time, and even after the third copy I don't think it made an awful lot of sense. It was my turn to get dinner that evening and I wrote between trips to the kitchen.

Dear Craddoc,

This is hard to write, but I won't be coming to see you over Easter vacation. I understand what you meant about our needing more time together and it hasn't anything to do with my being paranoid. I've grown out of that. And, I guess, out of some other things, too.

I gave you a bad time two years ago because I couldn't believe someone like you could really love me. I guess if you believe your mother doesn't love you when you're a little kid, it's hard to ever believe anyone else can. What's this? Psych 8 or 9?

Your choosing me made me feel like I was a person, and I thank you and will always love you for that. And this is real sad, Craddoc, but now we're both ready for new adventures — just not together. I never played you your love song as I

promised, and now I'm playing you "a
somebody done somebody wrong" song.
I know it doesn't help to say I'm sorry.
Elsie

I left the letter on my desk and went into
the kitchen to set the table and heat up frozen
peas. I didn't feel much like eating, but when
Sam and Mother came home, Sam gobbled up
the baked chicken, potatoes, peas, and fruit
salad.

When he was finished, he leaned back in his
chair. "That was superb! Say, I can't cook
much, but I can make waffles. How about I
make Sunday breakfast and take us all out to
dinner once a week for my turn with the
meals?"

Robyn and I exchanged glances. Maybe
having Sam around was going to be all right.
Mother sat there all rosy, looking about
twenty-five years old.

In the morning, I sealed up the letter and
dropped it in the mailbox on the way to
school.

"What was that?" Jenny asked when I
hopped back into the car.

"A 'Dear John' letter to Craddoc," I told
her.

"Sad, huh?" she said.

I nodded.

"Seems like the end of an era. I haven't got
a little brother or a daddy anymore and you
haven't got your football hero anymore. I
guess we aren't kids, either, anymore."

"Right," I said.

"What did you tell Craddoc?"

"I didn't tell him I knew I'd end up having to put up a fight like your mother if I kept letting him make my decisions."

"What about Jack?"

"I didn't say anything to him about Jack. He'll figure that out." I'd pulled into the student parking lot by then and we got out of the car together.

"That's sad, too," Jenny said.

I agreed.

I waited a week but there was no call from Craddoc, no letter. Sometimes in the night I wanted to explain to him over and over, "But I really did love you."

Gradually the guilt faded away and I grew lighter. Easter vacation. Easter vacation was coming closer. I couldn't repress a grin from seeping over my face while thinking about it.

"What are you looking so smug about these days?" Robyn wanted to know.

"I think I'll work at that Kalaloch Lodge this summer," I told her.

"How're you going to get the job?"

"I think I'll go visit Jack on Easter vacation and apply for the job then."

"By yourself?"

"That's right."

We were in the kitchen drinking cocoa together on this cold March afternoon. Robyn swirled the hot liquid with her spoon.

"What's Big Daddy Sam going to think about that?"

"That's something he'll have to figure out for himself."

"Does Jack know?"

"Not yet," I said as I drank the last of my cocoa and put my cup in the dishwasher, "but he's going to find out real quick. You got any stamps?"

Robyn found one in her purse, and as she gave it to me, she said, "I bet life with the redhead is going to be on a faster lane."

I took the stamp from her. "I bet you're right," I said, and headed for my bedroom to write letter number two.

About the Author

Barthe DeClements created the character of Elsie Edwards while she was teaching fifth grade. Her son provided the inspiration for Jack's adventures in *Seventeen & In-Between*. When he was barely out of his teens, Christopher worked as a timber faller and "cedar rat" on the Olympic Peninsula near the Queets Indian Reservation.

Ms. DeClements says, "On his trips home, Christopher regaled his family with tales of the wild loggers, an Indian sheriff, and a native Shaman. I imagined the Olympic Peninsula to be a place in which Elsie's friend Jack would thrive."

Barthe DeClements has worked as a school counselor, psychologist, and teacher. She lives in a log house, built by the youngest of her four children, on the Pilchuck River near Snohomish, Washington.